Jean Giono

Fragments of a Paradise

Translated from the French by
Paul Eprile

archipelago books

Library of Congress Cataloging-in-Publication Data available upon request.

ISBN 9781962770002

Archipelago Books
232 3rd Street #A111
Brooklyn, NY 11215
www.archipelagobooks.org

Distributed by Penguin Random House
www.penguinrandomhouse.com

Design by Gopa & Ted2, Inc.
Cover art: Odilon Redon, "Vision sous-meme" (c. 1900)
Frontispiece: Odilon Redon, "Dark Art and Craft"

This work received support for excellence in publication and translation from Albertine
Translation, a program created by Villa Albertine and funded by FACE Foundation.

This work is made possible by the New York State Council on the Arts with the
support of the Office of the Governor and the New York State Legislature.
Funding for the publication of this book was provided by a
grant from the Carl Lesnor Family Foundation.

This publication was made possible with support from
the National Endowment for the Arts

PRINTED IN CANADA

Introduction

J EAN GIONO WAS arrested and imprisoned at the beginning and at the end of World War II. His ostensible offense was pacifism, but his accusers thought he might be guilty of worse, even more unpatriotic crimes. In both instances they decided there was no real case against him and released him without further charge.

Long before these occurrences Giono, by then a well-known novelist, had written that France was "the wrong name" for the country that he and his friends loved, the place composed of landscapes and weather. He continued, "When I see a river I say 'river' when I see a tree I say 'tree'; I never say 'France.' That doesn't exist."[1] We may feel the wrongly named entity existed all too concretely in its interference in Giono's life, but his subtle argument goes deeper than surface history. It underlies an even larger claim made by his amazing book *Fragments of a Paradise,* written between the two imprisonments.

This work suggests that civilization doesn't exist. It is what Nietzsche

---

1. Jean Giono, *Jean le Bleu.* Grasset, 1932

called a "pretentious lie."[2] Or more modestly the achievements we group under headings like science, knowledge, culture, history, may marginally exist, but are devoted to error rather than to truth, and specialize in handing out the wrong names, leaving their victims afraid of being offered "a sort of lesson they were incapable of comprehending." In the book one of the reasons the captain of a vessel making a research expedition from European waters to the South Atlantic has chosen a sailing ship is that he doesn't "want to be dependent on coal yards, which would force me to set foot in civilized countries." He also says he thinks he and his crew "should sever all relations and ties with the civilized world."

Giono later said that this man's "philosophical side" was "disagreeable" and "false" and needed to be fixed but the reader may feel otherwise.[3] I am certainly moved and persuaded by his suggestion that he experiences "the anxiety that had gripped the modern world during the few years preceding my departure." We are not told the date of his ship's leaving Europe but it must be close to the time of the book's writing since one of the characters mentions the battle of Dunkirk (May to June 1940).

Giono tells us in a prefatory note to the *Fragments* that he dictated the text from August 6 to August 10, 1940. This information is very precise and also fictional, 'perfectly deceitful,' as his biographer Pierre Citron

---

2. Walter Redfern makes this connection to Nietzsche in his book *The Private World of Jean Giono*. Blackwell, 1967, p.91. The source is *The Birth of Tragedy and The Genealogy of Morals*, trans F. Golffing. Doubleday, 1956, p.53
3. Henri Godard, notes to *Oeuvres romanesques complètes*, vol 3. Gallimard, 1974, p.1546

says.[4] Giono did dictate the text to a secretary, Mlle. Alice, but the actual dates for that activity were February 18 to May 1, 1944. He published the book in 1948. It's important that we start with a fiction even before we get to the story, and that this move, paradoxically, takes us towards rather than away from reality. In a note addressed to himself Giono said "There are no imaginary worlds,"[5] and in a wonderful comment on the narrative structure of the work in question Henri Godard reminds us that "It is the captain who ... organizes the expedition ... But it is Giono who writes *Fragments of a Paradise.*"[6]

Giono noted on May 26, 1944, that he had "stopped work on *Fragments.*"[7] Had he abandoned his novel, or was his gesture "a way ... of saving the quest of his characters," as Derek Perrin suggests?[8] Pierre Citron says we should not believe we have been reading "fragments of an unfinished work ..."

> *Either the novel was conceived from the start as needing to look like a series of fragments or the term applies less to the text than to its contents: paradise exists on earth but is accessible only in fragments.*[9]

4. Pierre Citron, *Giono.* Editions du Seuil, 1990, p.370
5. Jean Giono, *Occupation Journal,* translated by Jody Gladding. Archipelago, 2020, p.191
6. Godard, p.154
7. *Occupation Journal,* p.207
8. Derek Perrin, *Jean Giono, itinéraire d'un homme sans Dieu.* Garnier, 2021, p.168
9. Citron, p.368

The book was meant, Giono says in his note, to "serve in due course as the basis for a poem." It is a poem – in prose and stylistically simulating a report on a scientific journey into the unknown. Almost the first thing we see in the text is a compass direction ("west-southwest") followed by the event of two boats dropping anchor in Madeira. There is a major source for this style, and Godard reports on it in detail. It is the naturalist Louis Roule's *L'Abîme des grand fonds marins* (*The Abyss of the Great Sea Depths*), published in 1934 as the seventh volume of a work called *Les Poissons et le monde vivant des eaux: études icthyologiques et philosophiques. (Fish and the Living World of Water: Studies in Ichthyology and Philosophy*). Giono's characters, like Roule, are very interested in squids and sperm whales. But there are literary sources too, above all Melville's *Moby Dick*, which Giono (with Joan Smith and Lucien Jacques) had translated into French in 1939. In *Fragments* we visit an abandoned cabin on the island of Tristan da Cunha which has in it, apart from some cooking pans and items of women's clothing, copies of *Don Quixote* in Spanish and *Paradise Lost* in English.

Quixote's eccentricities, which we may think of as acts of opposition to a too familiar world, haunt the *Fragments* in many ways, and Giono's journal reports eloquently on his sense of the importance of this book. For him *Don Quixote* is "not a satire on chivalry" but "an adieu to *grandeur*," as *Fragments* "must be an adieu to the poetic."[10] Perhaps Milton's subject alone would be enough to invite his inclusion but there are more specific

10. *Occupation Journal*, pp.6-7

connections. The central topic of *Fragments*, identified in its subtitle, is angels, and within the story, fallen ones. In his journal Giono mentions Breughel's painting of these figures, but the early parts of *Paradise Lost* also belong entirely to them. And the creation of monsters by Milton's God reads like a promotional blurb for a crucial scene in Giono's work:

> *There leviathan*
> *Hugest of living creatures, on the deep*
> *Stretched like a promontory sleeps or swims,*
> *And seems a moving land, and at his gills*
> *Draws in and at his trunk spouts out a sea.*[11]

In an interview Giono spoke of ships encountering "great fishes which rise from the bottom of the ocean, who are similar to angels."[12] The critic David Perrin shrewdly suggests that in *Fragments* "the sea becomes an inverted sky."[13] Members of the ship's crew catch sight of "a monstrous ray" swimming alongside the ship. It smells both "sweet" and "disgusting," and we are told that "despite their disgust, it was impossible to tear themselves away from the horrible and splendid spectacle." The crewmembers begin to discover, in their confusion, something of the real nature of their quest. "You felt like your soul was recoiling." Perhaps the angels' real job is to fall.

11. John Milton, *Paradise Lost*. Oxford, 2004, p.180
12. Jean Giono, *Entretiens*. Gallimard, 1990, p.114
13. Perrin, p.158

We read in the captain's journal that his project "isn't so much a voyage of exploration as it is a new way of life." He describes "the stated purpose" of the research journey in a way that immediately makes us feel he is about to reveal another one. It will engage in studies of "Zoology, Botany, Geology, Paleontology, Bacteriology, Hydrography, Oceanography, Meteorology, planetary Magnetism, atmospheric Electricity, and Gravity." The scholars on the ship do this, but the captain is after something else, closer to a secular theology than to science. It is in this context that he makes the remark I have already quoted about the modern world and continues:

> *I no longer have any interest in living under the conditions this*
> *era allows... It isn't possible that life can be only what we have*
> *experienced up until now. In spite of our scientific era and the*
> *advances we have made, it's undeniable that we're dying of bore-*
> *dom, of distress, and of poverty. I'm talking about a poverty of*
> *spirit and of a poverty of spectacle.*

At this point we have already heard a character in the book speaking of Hell and Arcadia and Paradise, and the narrator has told us, with a more than desperate irony, that only "two little, ridiculous words . . . to which no one attached any importance" will allow us to think about genuinely "mysterious things." The words are Hell and Heaven. It is at this point that the word "angel" becomes seriously active. A character says he is not an angel, and the captain replies that there are all sorts of angels. Returning to the topic the captain says, "Don't you believe that an angel might take the form of that monstrous fish that surfaced the other day?" We may be baffled by this reaching for religious imagery, but my sense is that this is just what Giono wants. The language is both familiar and remote, and in any case not reasonable. We are to use extravagant pictures of the unknown not to access the realms of dream or faith but to get ourselves ready for the really unknown, for the many forms of nature that can still surprise us and scare us. For what the captain calls our "first encounter with the real world."

The word "monster" and its family do a lot of interesting work in *Fragments*. A stormy sea is "monstrous" or "monstrously high." A giant squid is "monstrous." A seaman suggests that they should all imagine "a parallel order of grandeur, in which the monster isn't an exception, but something normal." It is this kind of thinking that induces, in the captain especially, the idea that the huge unforeseen fish may be angels. Immense, fallen, ugly, but proof that fragments of a paradise exist in the natural world. Of a paradise, we note. One among the possibilities.

When Giono said there are no imaginary worlds, he didn't mean we can't imagine things or places or people. He meant we don't have to. Reality, if we give it a chance, will catch up with the imagination and take us further. The captain says just this towards the end of *Fragments*: "Reality is more fantastic than imagination." Another character thinks "Nature itself isn't natural." These claims are not far-fetched in the light of what we have seen in Giono's pages, in his faux-realistic style and the monstrous objects he evokes: a cloud that turns into a massive bundle of birds, a sheet of ice that becomes the back of a vast squid. We don't have to take these fictions literally, but if we are to be faithful to Giono's extraordinary project, we need to understand and live with as much of their truth as we can. Perhaps that way we shall not, as the captain fears, find ourselves "perishing from pettiness and deadly boredom."

Michael Wood

FRAGMENTS OF A PARADISE

The reader will see later how the plot progresses further, what successes and failures the hero has, how he is to solve and overcome more difficult obstacles, what colossal images will emerge, how the hidden levers behind the wider story move, how its horizon opens up in depth and the whole story takes on a majestic lyrical flow.

—Gogol, *Dead Souls*

I will write, if only because, sadly, my times forbid me to.

—Alfieri, *Della Tirannida*

I

All the Preparations for Departure...

A LL THE PREPARATIONS for departure having been completed,
the two vessels set sail together on the 6th of July. On the 12th
of the same month, they were within sight of the last headland
of Europe, lying to their west-southwest at a distance of three nautical miles. On the 20th they passed two Spanish warships. One of them
fired a warning shot at *L'Indien*, obliging it to lower its sails; but once
the Spanish captain had come within hailing distance and learned that
the French vessels were setting out on a voyage of discovery on the high
seas, he made the appropriate apologies and took his leave politely, wish-
ing them bon voyage. On the 26th at 9:00 in the evening, *La Demoiselle*
and *L'Indien* dropped anchor in the harbor of Madeira, without further
incident.

Around 11:00 on the morning of the 28th, the breeze, fairly light but
steady until now, freshened with gusts from the west-northwest. The
anchor of *L'Indien* broke loose, and as it wouldn't take hold again, even
though they'd let out as much as 110 fathoms of cable, they weighed
anchor, set sail once more, and tacked around the roadstead. At 8:00 in

the evening they moored at another location, in 16 fathoms, over a bed of soft mud and shells. Three members of the crew who'd gone off in the big dinghy to collect water were missing on deck and didn't get back until the moment when the anchor was let go again.

The sea was grey and greenish, the way it is over great depths. When the sun went down, a broad expanse of sky lit up by increments, as if a wing of fire had slowly spread its feathers apart. The phenomenon was comprised of little, fluffy clouds, almost icy in appearance. They caught fire when they arrayed themselves, with a perceptible motion, in the expanse. The shafts of sunlight that illuminated them immediately made their structures—which really did resemble a bird's feathers—manifest. In this way the light was soon to be seen scattered across the entire expanse of the sky, so much so that, despite the late hour, an uncanny sort of daylight shone from all the points of the compass. Objects had no shadows, and the lapping of the sea, lit up in every direction, sounded like it was coming from a punch bowl.

During the night, torrents of rain began to fall. They could hear it chorusing from every ravine in the interior of the island. At half past midnight an ocean wave stove in four of the five windows of the great cabin, even though their shutters had been secured with Saint Andrew's crosses. The vessel heaved backward, as if it were foundering. A large storage chest—packed with salt and champagne—which was used as a table, broke free of its shackles. For a few moments the rolling of the ship made it tumble like a die. At last it swung open and the bottles spilled out, rolling and smashing against each other in an indescribable chaos. The carpenters worked through part of the night to fasten the chest back in place.

At daybreak some white and some copper-colored clouds were visible in the sky. The wind came out of the west, where the horizon was still a flaming red, as if the sun were intent on rising from that quarter. The east was completely dark. Despite these portents, the day was calm, though the sunlight remained murky and displaced.

The following day, aided by a gentle breeze from the south-southeast, the two vessels attempted once more to set sail and make headway; but an hour later the wind, after shifting in several directions, swung back to the west-southwest and the ships struggled to get back to the anchorage.

On the next day, the wind turned from north to northeast. They attempted again to take advantage of this, and *La Demoiselle* had already left the roadstead, when the incessant west wind returned, blowing stiff. They tried in vain to tack under full sail, but it was obvious that they were being pulled off course by the current, and at 4:00 in the afternoon they let themselves be drawn back to the anchorage yet again.

That evening at dusk, the same phenomenon appeared. There were no birds in the sky. The sea lay dead flat, and the silence was so profound, they could distinctly hear the voice of a shepherd calling out to the ships from the top of the coastal bluffs.

On the morning of the 3rd of August, tempted once more by a light north-easterly breeze, and following the example of a few fishing boats that had already set sail, the two vessels tried to do the same. The instant they rounded the cape, they were enveloped in a fog so thick, they could barely make out objects from one end of the ship to the other. Then the breeze subsided and they were becalmed yet again. Finally, around 2:00 in the morning, after a breeze had mounted gradually from the east, they were able to set course under full sail.

At 12:30 on the afternoon of the 5th of August, after winds varying in strength from several points of the compass, they sighted the northern-most of the Selvagens. From 4:00 to 6:00 they skirted along the east-ern side of the archipelago. They saw nothing but sheer cliffs, apparently inaccessible. The sea was crashing with fury against their walls. Number-less legions of birds were wheeling in the sky and flocking together in clouds. Then, as if stretched out by the wind, the flocks would disperse. In the slanting rays of the sun, they flashed sometimes with the dazzling colors of land birds, sometimes with the cold pallor of sea birds.

At 5:30 on the morning of the following day, at sunrise, they made out the entire mass of Tenerife through dense clouds. Propelled by a stiff breeze from the northeast, they soon rounded Point Neva. They were only a short distance from the harbor when the wind picked up again. They judged it best to wait for the gale to die down before heading to anchor in a spot that offered so little protection. The ship tacked back out to sea. But that evening the wind rose even higher. They spent the night under sail and lost sight of the island while they raced downwind on a day darkened by storms and reddened by lightning. They caught a glimpse of the island of Palma.

Three kingfishers were pursuing *L'Indien*. They sheltered in the wake of the ship during the rough weather.

II

The Northeasterlies

IN THESE VAST open spaces where nothing forced the wind to shift
or reverse, the northeasterlies prevailed across a broad front. They
moved uninterrupted like a rising tide. You could tell they blew at
extraordinary heights when a bird, smaller than the broad-winged predators that would attack it in due course, was swept away and lifted sky-
ward. The air was so clear, after the creature's frantic cry the very moment
the wind took hold of it, you could watch it gaining in altitude. The silent
black dot stayed in sight for a long while before it melted into the upper-
most regions.

In spite of its intensity, the power of the wind was so steady, it was still
possible to maneuver. But once you tried to imagine where its strength
could have arisen, you were forced to imagine vaster and vaster barren
stretches of ocean.

The roaring of this wind, after it had stopped up their ears, wrapped
the men in a deep solitude. The sea was barely ruffled. It rocked with a
long swell, almost flat, soundless; its motion was so extraordinarily lan-
guid, it showed only through flashes of iridescent color that ran suddenly

across its surface. Rising at regular intervals, the vessel fell at regular intervals, almost without a sound, except for the groaning of a few belaying pins that betrayed the straining of the hull timbers.

But as soon as they paid attention to this continuous roaring, which entirely filled the air, they realized it wasn't produced by the wind scouring over the sea. They could tell there was as much of a dull roar high up in the sky as there was on the water's surface. As soon as night fell, sudden and stark, the stars were so abundant and showed in so many sectors of the heavens all at once, they were like a squall of snowflakes.

Often, when the night sky was perfectly clear, they would see showers of impressively large, luminous meteors. Sometimes one of these meteors would appear at the zenith and leave an enormous streak, aligned from east to west, which turned into a wide, luminous band and remained visible for several minutes. Now they were forced to comprehend that the roaring of the wind arose from its huge totality whirling around the earth.

As soon as daylight returned and they faced this limitless immensity, they were conscious, right away—with no need to reflect—that beyond the visible horizon, the barren stretch of ocean was hemmed in by another curve. And so, despite how fast they were making headway, they had an enormous feeling of immobility and suspense.

Only the whistling of the shrouds and sheets continued to give any sensation of a habitable world, and the swaying of a cable and its snapping against the mast were a comfort to the spirit. But suddenly the mainsails were sagging and luffing and the jibs were beating like drums. The yawing of the ship and the abrupt billowing of the sails, the loud creaking of all the stays, the groans coming from deep in the hull: all these revealed the violent forces they faced. At times, though nothing was disturbing the smooth undulation of the sea, a sharper sound began singing from up ahead across the expanse. The further on they sailed, the louder the sound became. Little by little it divided into parts, into modulations and rhythms, until they saw the tip of a mountainous island loom above the water.

As the ship got closer, the peaks and crags were scraping like bows on the long strings of the wind and making them vibrate in the depths of the valleys. The sailors could hear some tree-wrack crackling. During the time they skirted along the coast, the wind enveloped the ship in every kind of terrestrial sound. This was a great relief. They were suddenly conscious of things at a human scale.

But gradually, as the ship sped away, it left these pleasing sounds behind one by one, and it wasn't long before the men were pent up once again in the vast solitude.

For many days on end the sky remained completely empty.

Every night the coming of darkness covered the ship in a luminous snowsquall, and every morning the men searched the skies for any remnants of celestial wreckage they could cling to. It was only after they'd waited a long while that a feathery wisp of icy cloud would break the line of the horizon. Often it would drop down right away as if it had been the spouting of some distant whales. The men needed to stay on watch constantly to keep their hopes up. Sometimes, after the wisp had appeared, a whole fan of pinions would go on spreading, and the sun would ignite them with dazzling colors. But as the cloud-wings were deploying, the anguish of solitude and the anxiety of the unknown would start to shroud the men's hearts. What could they be, these monstrous birds that were sure enough of their plumage to be able to open it this wide in the face of such superhuman force! It would have been a relief to see the actual body of the monster appear, but the wind went on pounding it at will, and often by midday it was nothing more than a shapeless squall that raced ahead of the ship, gnashing at the sea in an angry downpour.

The wind had an awful smell. It was difficult to discern, because it was overpowering and pervasive. Even so, it got right up your nose and onto your tongue and you tasted it in your saliva. Under the shapeless, spotless azure of the daytime sky, when you were blinded by the countless fires glinting from the patches of foam and the sharp crests of the waves, you wanted night to come. It seemed that the hint of violet, which began by darkening the water's surface and then spread until it blackened the whole of the east, was the bearer of calm and security. But it wasn't long before this state of ease gave way to the uninterrupted, endless howling that filled the entire realm of sky and sea.

So it was the wind they were smelling. It had a salty taste: a little musky, not unpleasant, but it gave you a ferocious appetite for rocks, cliffs, and a boundless interior where you could at last feel solid ground underfoot. When the darkened east spread its shadow over the waves; when it engulfed the body of the ship and extinguished the reflections and foam that lay ahead; when it swiftly shrouded the gilded whiteness of the sails of *La Demoiselle*: then the anguish of having nothing firm to rely on held everyone in its grip.

Now the wind started drumming out a tom-tom on enormous gourds. In spite of what the maps showed; in spite of the steady, unobstructed breeze; in spite of the void through which they'd been plying without end, and the void the prow was cleaving ahead, so vast and deep it seemed to yawn like a dizzying height; in spite of all this, they could hear the wind pounding on distant islands. It landed with regular blows, with sonorities that made the sailors' stomachs turn. In this way a regular, implacable pattern of drumbeats was locating tiny pieces of land that were lost in the immensity. The sailors were passing through the midst of these islets, blindly, unable to cry for help. It was even more terrible to have to acknowledge the impossible existence of these islets, and their tremendous remoteness as figments of the imagination.

The glassy rollers chafed ceaselessly against the sides of the ship.

But not long after, the wind started to beat on even gloomier drums. It pummeled the abysses and its power succeeded in drawing rumblings, in which it was impossible to find the least sign of hope, out of all the depths.

Sometimes, despite the dark, you could see the impact of this huge, invisible hand. From on board you glimpsed a colorless patch a few cable lengths away. This patch would come crashing down onto the waves and spray and abruptly light up with ember-like phosphorescence. After a second or two, during which you instinctively held your breath, the sound the impact had loosed would mount up from the depths. It was a tangible sound like the wind itself, and while you listened you could hear the walls of the ship moaning. And then a new smell would add itself to the smell of the wind. It was a smell of open sea. It wasn't connected to anything you could possibly have known. There was nothing cheerful about it. It deepened your sense of aloneness because it spoke of things that were totally unfamiliar, things that had nothing in common with humanity. It could just as well have been the smell of a huge animal, or a huge plant, or a huge deity. It could just as well have been the smell of sweat, or claws, or teeth, or mouths, but it was impossible to imagine anything it was actually connected to. There was only one thing for certain: it was a smell of life.

It added terribly to the feeling of being alone, and you realized you were part of something unknown, something you would never know, and it was useless to make overtures or deferential bows toward it. The destiny that until now you thought you could shape, or control, or gently steer, you now understood was in no way susceptible to human powers. Abruptly, you knew for a fact that everything you had done up until the present moment, and everything you could expect to do until you died, was essentially minuscule. The power you'd often put to the test, the spirit that could face up to the greatest extremes in the world, you understood it was feeble, and that up until now you'd been totally blind. Even death, against which you never stopped struggling day in day out, in order to carry on: now you knew death didn't have the dimensions you'd assumed until now, not at all.

The defenses you'd thrown up against death were turned inside out and engulfed by this flood, more powerful than the sea, and denser than this snowsquall of stars.

The wind, repeating the blows it was landing on the faraway islands and the abyss, kept drumming out, without letup, the same melancholy music that gave no reason for either hope or despair. While, at the same time every evening, when the wind freshened enough for you to feel it filling the jibs, the deck began to give way under your feet. A sort of sonorous magic made the remote, uplifted islands sing, along with their trees; the abysses and bottomless troughs deepened, and the ship seemed to be suspended each time it pitched downward. There was no dramatic show of the wind's power, but a sort of calm and eternal certainty. This was not a romantic display of cosmic attitudes. Everything showed itself as a fact, and the sound of the gongs allowed this fact to dominate at all times.

Now the days and nights were calm and beautiful. The ship was easy to steer. The course gave no cause for concern. But all the routes they'd plied until now, in countless regions, in pursuit of happiness and back again, were erased from everyone's memory. The ease now afforded to the crew gave each member the time to consider and reconsider, without growing weary, the most important aspects of their lives.

On *L'Indien* the captain started to curse. Calmly. At his pipe. At his lighter. At a button on his tunic. Just for the fun of it. The officers were cursing, but not in anger, and the crew began to indulge in the sheer pleasure of cursing. One evening when the moon was out, Hourdeau, on the night watch, went looking for the cabin boy, who'd gone to sleep on a stack of tarpaulins. He wondered where that little fool had gotten to. Then Hourdeau went below, took off his boots, and started to curse, calmly. First at the candle. Then at a flask of rum in the pocket of his pea-coat. He went back up on deck, not worried, simply wanting to find the cabin boy. He called to him to windward. As it left his mouth, the boy's name had no substance. It was immediately torn away. But what had real substance, and hit just the right note, was an old swear word he recalled, which he started to repeat with glee.

The cabin boy had hidden himself behind a coil of rope. He was sitting with his knees raised, his arms wrapped around them, his head resting on his right arm. He'd tried out all the swear words he'd learned from the crew, methodically, one by one, gauging their weight and their worth. Next, he tried inventing more curses, intently searching for the dirtiest words, the most violent filth. For a long while he'd held back from mixing these obscenities with the name of God. But the moon was devouring the clouds, and the wind, ever more uninhibited, made the depths rumble right beside him; so now the cabin boy mixed the names of God and the Virgin with every one of the foul and obscene words he was capable of remembering. His teeth chattered and he cried. He was cold and he felt lost. He was afraid from one moment to the next that he wouldn't have enough strength to come up with the foulest obscenity of all.

III

They Observed That...

THEY OBSERVED that *La Demoiselle* rode the waves exceptionally well and was rapidly outsailing *L'Indien*. The captain signaled the other ship to heave to, and he sent the small dinghy across with special orders granting *La Demoiselle* the freedom to chart its own course. He fixed the Bay of Good Success in the Strait of Le Maire as their rendezvous. *La Demoiselle* would await them there and begin taking observations, researching plants and animals, and thoroughly overhauling its gear and navigational instruments. When the dinghy had returned to *L'Indien*, *La Demoiselle* raised its pennants in salute. After receiving the signal for safe travels, it wasted no time exploiting its advantages under full sail, in a fair breeze. On the 8th of August toward nightfall, it could no longer be sighted from *L'Indien*'s bow.

On the 16th at 8:00 in the evening, *L'Indien* witnessed a bright meteor, broad in diameter and bluish in color. It was accompanied by a feline purring, which for a minute rose higher than the sound of the wind. The fireball plunged fast toward the northwest, and from the spot where it dropped into the ocean, a long, green shaft of light shot up and remained visible in the sky for many hours.

At noon on the 17th even though all the charts showed a vast stretch of open sea, they saw a swallow following the ship. In the evening it perched in one of the gun-ports. While they were shifting the sails they disturbed it, and it went and sheltered in the stern ornaments.

For the next two days it continued to flutter around the ship. The next day they spotted bonitos and dolphins in pursuit of flying fish. The latter would shoot out of the water to evade their predators. When the flying fish skimmed close to the surface and encountered the crest of a wave, they'd shoot through and resume their flight on the other side. There were several huge schools of these fish. Some of them shot too high and landed, exhausted, on the deck of the ship. The dolphins, and the bonitos—the most beautiful fish in the sea—frolicked in immense blossoms of foam. Sometimes they reared up, standing almost on their tails, and their skin would glisten like metallic shards. They submerged without a sound into the pitch-dark water, and you could watch them, fledged like arrows and lit up with spume, covering long stretches of the sea. Bunches of bubbles, like clusters of grapes, followed the movements of their tails.

On the 20th toward midday the rain poured down in torrents. This deluge soaked the plumage of the poor swallow that had been accompanying *L'Indien* for several days. It was forced to land on the aftercastle and let itself be caught. After they'd dried it off, they set it free to fly through the passageway and into the great cabin. It adapted to its prison and soon went after the large population of flies. At noon they opened the windows and the bird regained its freedom. But at 6:00 in the evening it flew back into the passageway and the cabin. It ate more flies, then took off again to perch for the night on the exterior of the vessel. The next day, emboldened by the peaceful existence it was enjoying, it risked flying back in through the gun ports and the hatches.

It spent a part of the morning, untroubled, in the middle of Monsieur Vignal's cabin. But after it left, they didn't see it again. It's likely that it ended up in the berth of one of the sailors, who killed it to feed to his cat. Since there was no land anywhere nearby, it must have been a bird that had been aboard *La Demoiselle*, and then been shooed away while the two ships were next to each other.

On the 26th toward 8:00 in the morning a huge yellow bird fell out of the air, exhausted, right in front of the ship's cook. He was smoking his pipe at the top of the galley ladder. At the very moment when the bird landed on deck, he thought he saw a big flame shoot up beside it. He was still deeply affected. The bird, barely breathing and making only a few, nervous twitches, did in fact look like an amazing, flaming object. You could spread its wings without any effort, as though it were dead. In the sunlight, they took on all the colors from red to violet, like flames from dry firewood. A few spasms marked the desperate efforts it was making to breathe by inflating its crop. These spasms also revealed, underneath its fiery yellow plumage, the bright red glow of its feathery down. The bird heated your hand intensely when you lifted it up. The men debated what kind of bird it might be. Monsieur Hour, the naturalist, maintained it was a sort of Roller, basing his assertions on the little blue-green tufts that swept back like acanthus leaves above its eyes and draped, like the feathered crest of a helmet, onto its nape.

The creature died in Monsieur Hour's hands, and he took it away to paint a watercolor of the specimen before he stuffed it. He'd already kept it in his cabin for two or three days, and had made a very precise drawing, when the corpse of the bird disappeared. Since the portholes of the taxidermy room had been secured with iron cross-braces, it was impossible to imagine that a gust of wind had swept the remains into the sea. As well, cats, which several of the seamen kept in their hammocks, were never allowed in this part of the ship. When the crew was questioned, no one admitted to having snatched the bird.

A few days later the cook had reason once again to go into raptures. At dusk he'd come to the rail to fill a firkin with seawater, which he took down to the hold. A little later two sailors, who were idling down below, heard some cries and went to investigate. They found the cook on his knees in front of the firkin, astonished by what he was seeing: a tiny creature with a pointed head, its body about one centimeter thick and three or four in length, with a black patch at one of its extremities. It was opal in hue, but abruptly turned purple, a purple so unusual and intense that you couldn't imagine ever having seen that color anywhere before. This phenomenon was accompanied, or perhaps produced, by a slight contraction that caused the animal to rise to the surface. At the moment it was about to touch the surface, its color abruptly transformed into a sort of blue, a blue so intense it looked like a tiny speck of night sky caught inside the firkin. Now, two little spots of light appeared on the animal's head. They were so vibrant, you had the impression they were sending out rays. At this point, the animal descended to the depths of the bucket. When it reached bottom, it turned such an exquisite green that the sailors themselves couldn't hold back exclamations of surprise. Then, after a convulsion that looked as though it would make it explode, it faded and rose, grey and lifeless, back to the surface.

The spectacle had been so radiant and so rapid that the three men remained awestruck for a long while. What had made the phenomenon extraordinary, above all, was the intensity of the colors, rather than the mimicry itself. Indeed, as they told each other, none of the three men had ever seen anything, anywhere, resembling the colors they'd just seen. One of them even claimed that, during the phases when the hues were changing, there'd been an explosion of more, new colors that had no name in any language.

All three of them came up carrying the firkin, then went back to the rail to repeat this miraculous harvest from the sea. They realized it was quite easy to fish for creatures of this kind; the water near the ship was covered with them. You could even see them in dense shoals that must have been several meters thick. The profusion of fireworks that burst out incessantly in the shoal rendered the three men incapable of containing their exclamations and shouts. Monsieur Hour, drawn by the commotion, took up his position next to them and remained, as he himself put it, stunned by the spectacle, for so long that he completely forgot about his scientific duties.

The other officers and crew, attracted by these enthusiastic shouts, went so far as to leave off executing a minor maneuver, in order to come and look on. Monsieur Laborderie took it upon himself to inform the captain. It was at this point that Monsieur Hour, coming to his senses, had them lower the firkin again to bring up some more specimens of the animal.

This time, four of five of these tiny creatures were caught. They were bunched together so tightly that at first the men thought they were a single animal. But the creatures separated and each one began to display its colors on its own. Arrayed like this, they formed such a vivid rainbow, the men's cries of wonder grew even stronger.

They spent almost a whole hour drawing firkins full of these little creatures up onto the deck. Once their explosions of fireworks ended, they turned grey.

Monsieur Hour tried to keep one alive in a water glass, but during the night the specimen decomposed so completely that by morning it was nothing more than a drop of syrup.

Nevertheless, the cook, who continued to be joyful and secretive all day, finally admitted that he'd succeeded in keeping one of these animals alive. He staunchly resisted Monsieur Hour's desire to examine it scientifically in order to determine its species. All he would allow him to do was to come and confirm the fact with his own eyes. The cook claimed that anyone could succeed the way he had: it was simply a matter of dropping a grain of pure salt into the water. And he proved exactly right.

In the following days he maintained that, using this system, you could keep these creatures alive indefinitely, and they'd go on producing magical colors without interruption. Eventually Monsieur Hour determined the organism to be a parasite of jellyfish. Once this had been established, and since it wouldn't be feasible to keep a specimen alive for the entire length of the voyage, even if the water were salted regularly, he threw the one he'd kept for study back into the sea. The cook held on to his. Every evening he'd draw a stool close to his berth and place the glass containing the creature right next to his bed. In this manner he'd spend hour upon hour, during which you could hear him shouting excitedly in Basque dialect. But, for the most part, he emerged from these meditations in a profound state of melancholy.

On September 1st they spotted a number of dolphins. And then they suddenly noticed a big fish alongside, which perfectly resembled what the Dutch call a "devil fish." From its outward appearance, you would have taken it to be a member of the genus of rays, but it seemed to be a new species.

On September 3rd they noticed several cetaceans passing close by the vessel. They were heading north and northwest. They looked like dolphins. But the men were surprised that they weren't cavorting as they usually do. They seemed to be fleeing in a straight line. They passed right next to the hull at top speed, rocking from side to side and rolling around, with their mouths wide open to shoot through the waves with more control. This rapid swiveling motion repeatedly exposed their white bellies. During the whole time they were going by, flashes of white and bubbling spume covered the sea with sparkling reflections. The next day they observed a large number of flying fish fleeing in the same direction.

They were mingled with bonitos, from which they were no longer trying to escape.

On September 8th the ship's prow ran into an amazing cluster of sea anemones. On the same day, two or three times, the crew mentioned they could smell something. And soon there was an undeniable sugary smell in the air. This was subtle at first, but it rapidly became cloying. The very next day, the smell was so intense, it caused some of the men to feel a peculiar sort of dread followed by weariness and nausea.

They sailed for three days in a steady breeze. But, on the morning of the 18th, they abruptly came upon a stretch of calm water, and by 8:00 in the evening the smell was so hard to bear, they were at a loss what to do.

Monsieur Hour suggested fumigating with lavender. This afforded some relief, but for no apparent reason, the cabin boy immediately started weeping.

Some other members of the crew also exhibited their dissatisfaction. When it was explained to them that it was necessary to get rid of the stench by any means, they answered that they agreed; but that they would prefer to make use of one of the chemical agents, of which there were plenty in the hold, rather than spread the terrestrial scent of lavender, which reminded them in a most unwelcome way of pure, invigorating mountain air. What's more, the captain shared their opinion. So, they placed packets of chlorine on the deck; they even started to spray their clothes with bleach.

Since the calm conditions were leaving the crew with nothing to do, almost all the men came up on deck. The sea was exceptionally still. As far as the eye could see, it was as flat as a sheet of frozen metal, smooth as a slick of oil without the slightest ripple. The ship was so becalmed, the water met the hull in a precise line without a crease.

It was in this situation that the ship seemed to run aground, with so much violence that a few men tumbled head over heels on deck. There was indescribable alarm and dismay, but the vessel steadied right away. Such a silence fell, you could hear the masts vibrating at their tips, where the tremor that ran through the ship had just died out.

Now the men who were looking over the port side began letting out muffled cries. The flat sea was reflecting a blinding sun, like a mirror. But on the port side, which was in shadow, if you looked down perpendicularly right next to the vessel, it was possible to see some distance into the water. The men weren't even paying attention to the smell—which had intensified in a strange way and was getting stronger by the minute—because a frightening presence had started to rise up through this visible part of the depths.

Those who were first to spot the thing said afterwards that they'd seen, at first, far beneath the surface where the waters grew dark, some golden-brown shimmerings of the sort you see in coal tar. They hadn't been paying them much attention, when they saw a kind of white light, blinding like a snowbank in bright sunshine, burst out silently in the deep. This white light faded immediately, turned red, purple, then violet, then blue, and then into that new, unknown color they'd seen already in the little sea creature taken prisoner by the cook.

The men let out stifled cries as soon as they perceived that these flashes of color were coming from the skin of an animal so huge, you could see them extending over an area greater than a square mile. What's more, in spite of the glaring of the sun, the flaring of the huge animal was just as visible to starboard as well. You could easily tell that the creature was rising to the surface.

While they were all leaning over the rail in astonishment, and it was impossible to imagine an evasive maneuver of any kind, they felt the ship shivering from stem to stern, no longer from a shock, but from a prolonged caress. At the same time, the seething colors and flashes were illuminating the sea to such a depth, it was possible to make out the swaying of tall seaweeds and the furtive passage of huge blue sea snails far down below. The flares began to move forward, and soon, while the sides of the ship were growing dark, they could see that the surface ahead, which remained incredibly smooth, was becoming colored over a vast expanse with silken reflections.

A minute later, without there having been a hint of a breeze, the flat surface of the sea rose into a dome more than two meters high. For a brief moment, it formed a sort of vault, which stayed incredibly smooth.

In dread, they gauged that the arc into which the sea was forming was at least two hundred meters across and more than three meters tall at its apex. Obviously, this happened very quickly, and right away the foaming waters parted around a mound of skin that, as soon as it met sunlight, turned with amazing rapidity from blue to a purplish red.

While the vessel was making tremendous yaws, one of which threatened to submerge the starboard deck, the animal was stretched out ahead of them, motionless, for a few hundred meters.

They could tell that this was a monstrous ray, similar to the ones they'd encountered on September 1st, but this one was more than a hundred and fifty meters wide. It calmly blew out a spout of water, which rose for several meters before it tumbled down and slapped the leathery skin on the creature's back. Then the ray stayed still, and the waves it had set in motion washed against the length of its dorsal cartilages. It let itself be rocked and carried along by this tide.

The sweet, disgusting smell had become so intense, a few of the men began to vomit, despite the chlorine they'd spread right away on the deck and crushed under their boots.

But, despite their disgust, it was impossible to tear themselves away from the horrible and splendid spectacle. The creature looked like it was soaring slowly over the surface of the sea, like an eagle in flight. With a simple flexing of its huge, cartilaginous wings, it built up a turbulence that lifted its head out of the water. On its skin, which the slapping of the spout had revealed to be the toughest kind of hide, each movement produced countless colors and flashings, like the kind that play across the feathers of birds flying in the open air. Waves, which started out gold, were arising from the almost imperceptible quivering at the edges of the ray's wings. They then extended over the whole of the animal's body in an unvarying sequence that passed from purplish red to royal blue, to violet, and finally to that unknown color the men's eyes could never get enough of, which filled their hearts with a magnificent, unprecedented sorrow.

When these bursts of color, which rose up from both sides of the creature, reached the middle of its back—where there was a bristling of horns as tall as a man—the whole fish became coated with a sort of golden carapace so luminous it made the daylight appear grey. This radiance cast harsher shadows than the sun.

While the creature remained spread out on the surface, waves of color passed across it continuously. Now that the men were riveted by the spectacle and it was impossible to tear their eyes away from it, even to vomit, they could detect, amongst the four familiar colors—red, blue, violet, and yellow—an infinity of unknown colors. The impression they gave couldn't be conveyed in words. These hues flowed between the other colors, combined with them, transformed one into the other through a countless number of fleeting modulations, each possessing an unspeakable, awe-inspiring power to provoke revulsion. Sometimes they were so eruptive they obscured the known colors and the men were left, though they were still wholly alive, going through transformations of the kind you can expect to pass through after death.

Monsieur Hour had simply gone in search of an automatic pistol.

After an incalculable lapse of time, they could tell the animal's head was beginning to go under, and the sea was rising forward along the length of its back. Little by little, in slow motion, the giant ray rolled over head first and began to slide toward the depths, making no disturbance or sound, like oil poured into oil. At last, as it was disappearing, it abruptly raised a huge, spear-like tail more than twenty meters into the air. Its underside suddenly displayed, in a flash, a fresh pink color like a woman's flesh. Its appearance caused the crew to emit a stifled groan.

A moment later the surface lay unbroken, and the vessel received a sharp, direct shock across its keel, like the blow from an ax head. They hurried to inspect for damage while the stays were still creaking, but there was no lasting effect except for a remarkable revulsion that held everyone in its grip. Right away spirits and rum were handed out, but until nightfall the whole crew didn't stop heaving with nausea, and when the captain came on deck, he showed a sickly, pale cast under his beard. At dawn the following day, a fresh breeze enabled them to set full sail.

They started talking about the smell. It was no longer in the air, but remained nestled in the folds of their wool undershirts. The men hadn't been frightened by the creature. They'd been stunned by its size, amazed by the show of colors. But if they'd been given the order to attack it, they would have done so. To tell the truth, they'd all been expecting this order. It was significant, if absurd, that Monsieur Hour had run to fetch his automatic pistol. But they went on and on talking about the smell. They came up with the explanation that the ray must spend its days sprawled out over the silty deposits on the ocean floor. However, some of the sailors could see no clear reason why these deposits should have a nauseating smell. The men also tried to figure out where else they might have encountered the same offensive odor. Some of them maintained you could pick up the same smells in the vicinity of rundown abattoirs and rendering plants. But the others answered them right away, saying that this smell had a certain, undeniable charm, a charm that was not to be found—far from it—in those other sorts of smells.

And it was true: at first, when the wafts were still faint and getting lost in the shifting winds, they'd recalled the fragrance produced by large fields of narcissi in full bloom. No one could deny that the men had yearned for the smell in the beginning and that the feeling it had initially aroused in them was one of joy and inner contentment. It wasn't even the intensity of the smell that made it revolting, because, in the very midst of the nausea it provoked, there was still that intimation of flowers in bloom. The revulsion arose more from a profound disappointment than from a blow to the senses. You felt like your soul was recoiling.

The men on watch discussed the matter thoroughly and concluded that they were sick, above all, from anxiety. That was it, absolutely. They'd given it some serious thought. True, behind the honeyed sweetness of the smell, you felt something that made you think of carrion and decay. But this feeling was purely imaginary. It was an impression, rather than an actual smell, that you were getting. As the sweetness grew more and more intense and sugary, you really did end up thinking of those streams of putrefaction that pour from the drains of abattoirs, or of the stench that emanates from rendering plants. But the real smell was still a scent of narcissus, of jonquil, and of jasmine. In reality, and this was what they settled on, it was a disturbing smell. On this, everyone agreed. It was even more disturbing because its effect was inexplicable. A blind man who smelled this odor would feel uneasy in his soul. And, in this regard, they could point to an example: Noël Guinard, the storekeeper. Since the start of the voyage, whether it was rainy or windy, whether by day or by night, he had not emerged from his hold. They hadn't seen him on deck even once. Down in his storeroom, in between the crates and the rows of canned preserves, he'd set up a magnificent cubbyhole. He was a skinny, dark-complexioned, crookbacked man with reddened eyes, narrow shoulders, weak hands and legs, armed for life with only a prodigious memory and an even more prodigious sense of order. He was the very personification of order. In his vicinity, and within the entire range of his movements, nothing could stray from its place. Not only did he assign things their places once and for all, but he remembered each one infallibly, and you couldn't imagine anything that would make him forget it. In this way he was rightly considered the uncontested master of provisions and of everything that needed to be organized and kept track of. He'd already made several voyages with the captain, and, ever since, the captain couldn't imagine keeping things in order without him. The rest of the crew was familiar with his ways. They knew that to make him lose sight, for just one second, of the organization he was in charge of, was a torture you couldn't possibly want to inflict on him. As soon as he'd come on board, he slid down into this shadowy underworld. And no one had seen him emerge from it since. They'd forgotten about him; they would have forgotten about him even in the midst of a shipwreck, he'd taken such care to disappear into his arrangements. His contacts with the rest of the crew, with the officers, with the captain, were made through a cabin boy. Guinard would send the requisitions through this boy, who would summon the detachments responsible for carrying staples to the cook and delivering other provisions to the quartermaster for distribution. Of course, when the winged creature had surfaced ahead of them, no one cared whether Noël Guinard had come up on deck. They were certain he hadn't come up, and the cabin boy confirmed it. They knew, too, that it would have taken a lot more than the sort of ax blow the ship had sustained when the animal submerged again, to make Guinard leave his hideout. But, a few days later, the boy brought some important news: Guinard hadn't been worried about the smell. The other men wondered if it had disrupted the storekeeper's routine. The boy made it clear that, naturally, he hadn't failed to tell him the minutest details of the monster's appearance and behavior. But, according to the boy, during this whole time, Guinard wasn't paying any attention to him or to what he was saying. Right away the storekeeper had plunged into a kind of stocktaking more monstrous than the beast itself, or at least equal to it in monstrosity, which consisted of confirming, with extraordinary precision, all of his established arrangements.

It seemed that, once this had been done, Guinard remained in a sort of stupor so intense that, for a whole day, he forgot to light his lantern. Now, the boy said, it looked like he was down there drawing some sort of symbol on a piece of cloth. The boy couldn't explain things any more clearly. The silence in the shadows had scared him so badly, they had to give him a glass of rum. All he could tell them was that, at that very moment, Guinard had lit a candle and was drawing with ink in a corner of his hideout. Seamen third class Archigard and Paumolle, who'd come off the previous watch, decided to go and take a look at these antics. They came back saying, in their own words, it had been easy to catch Guinard in the act. They'd come right up to him and seen what he was doing. He was drawing a cross on a heart-shaped piece of cloth he'd cut out of some shirting material. When they asked him what it was, he told them plainly, it was a scapular.

This became the sole topic of conversation on the forecastle. It was agreed without further question that these goings-on were altogether laughable. However, the sailors were unanimous in allowing there really was something about what they'd experienced that made the storekeeper's handiwork reasonable, up to a point. Little by little they managed to figure out what had made the smell so sickening. And leading seaman Savourin Baléchat, a native of La Cadière in the Var, who'd graduated first in his class from the Toulon lycée, concluded, in a peculiar fashion, that he understood the true nature of the emotion they'd all felt. He put it in a rather strange way: in his opinion, it was an *anti-Arcadian* sentiment. He had to elaborate. He said that, in other words, it was something that denied the existence of *Arcadia* and *Paradise*. This, of course, left everyone dumbfounded. He then explained in a way they could all understand, asking if each of them didn't have a secret recess where he kept a close guard over his own private visions of tranquility; whether these involved a wife, a mother, a child, a house, a home, a garden, an orchard, a mistress, or, more crudely yet, intoxication in whatever form, even bingeing or carousing; in short, every sort of joy, of good fortune, of longing for what life ought to bestow on everyone. And they did say to him, now that he put it this way, that they vaguely understood; that, in general, in this part of your soul you did store up images of all the things that could transform your life into a sort of earthly paradise. Sometimes what you want to get out of this store of images doesn't amount to a lot. But it's this "not a lot" that really matters. If you're always deprived—if you no longer have any hope of possessing this "not a lot" that actually matters—you are, strictly speaking, in what we call Hell. And this store of tranquil images was what he himself called Arcadia and Paradise.

They understood perfectly what he meant, and this led to a long silence on the forecastle.

It was evening, and the steady wind gave absolutely no reason for concern. A crown of purple encircled the ship.

When Baléchat tried to explain further, they told him quite abruptly they'd understood. Everyone agreed. It was, in fact, exactly this mysterious feeling that had caused all of their revulsion. For confirmation, a few of the men tried to find a trace of the smell in the folds of their undershirts; and once they'd found it and compared it with their mysterious Arcadia, they threw back their heads, their eyes vacant, a bitter taste in their mouths.

Now someone spoke about the colors. It was inconceivable that even the most splendid hue in the known spectrum could have been novel enough to impress mariners who, having spent their lives roaming from Greenland to Tierra del Fuego, had sailed under thousands of auroral arches. So, they talked neither of that indigo, nor of that purple, nor of that emerald with which the monster had arrayed itself, but of that remarkable, unknown color, and of that infinity of new, nameless colors that had held all the known colors together.

On the following day they saw a dorado. It was around four o'clock in the afternoon. A steady northeasterly was blowing, allowing them to make good headway. Some of the men were fishing from the stern, with lines that had been handed out to them that morning, for a little diversion from their routine. They were leaning over the bubbling wake, and from there they saw this dorado calmly following the ship, at a depth of a few meters. What impressed them most was the ease with which the creature swam. At this hour the sun had started to drop toward the horizon and was striking the smooth rollers with slanting rays. Underneath the surface of the water, it was lighting up a landscape, and the shadowy depths were its firmament. All the fish's charm and skill were being displayed in this opalescent realm. The dorado's golden exterior was plainly visible, and the sunlight didn't fail to deflect sparkling beams off its scales. Even so, it was the skillfulness of its movements, and of the arabesques it traced along its course, that aroused the interest of the sailors most of all. In fact, not only did it keep up effortlessly with the brisk progress of the ship, but also, with unimaginable agility, it launched into such rapid spirals and knots, circles and angles, that they remained inscribed as golden trails in the sea.

In the forecastle that evening, when they'd started talking again about the colors of the monstrous ray, one of the sailors began disputing and carrying on about the movements of the dorado. He did this with such vehemence, and his body so closely imitated his speech, he was almost dancing.

For a while toward noon each day, they were followed by sharks. Not the biggest variety, but from what they could see, they guessed they were about two to three meters long. The sailors cast them a heavy hook covered in rancid fat. The line was set to drag astern and tied off securely with a long rope. It hadn't been in the water for more than a minute or two before one of the creatures tore at it in a spiraling rush and bit with such violence, they could see the iron point of the hook, covered in red, pierce right through its upper jaw. As soon as it felt itself caught and dragged, the creature thrashed around furiously, revealing its true size. It might have been almost six meters long. Twisted into a circle, like a bangle pinched between two fingers, it made a huge leap and crashed back into a cloud of bloody seawater. They let it dive, but it wasn't long before it resurfaced and, worn out and half-drowned, it trailed along in the wake like a corpse. Now they began hauling it in with the windlass, and although it stayed inert during the whole operation, when it flopped down onto the deck it started striking the rail with amazing violence. But the sailors had already armed themselves with sharp axes, and while they leapt about to avoid the blows of the frenzied tail, they began to hack the live shark into pieces. With two ax blows, Hervéou separated the body from the tail, and an oar they'd placed inside the shark's jaws was ground to a pulp by its triple rows of teeth. It was extremely dangerous to stay within reach of the separated parts. The rope it was bound with could hardly restrain the convulsions of the severed beast. They dragged it to the forecastle. It was hoisted and sliced open. Being experienced in this sort of exercise, Hervéou and Marchais took care of the operation. Their expressions grim, they answered the monster's twisting and turning with jeers and taunts. They tore out the intestines and the heart. Two hours later this heart was still beating so violently, anyone who tried to grab it and hold on to it in their hands was forced by its unpredictable pulses to let it go. Its mutilated remains, kept immersed in water to prevent them from spoiling, were still showing signs of life the following day.

If the spectacle of this tenacious life had affected the sailors, they would have an even more disturbing topic to discuss afterwards. Because, in the course of the day, they heard stifled groans and exclamations coming several times from the galley. Since the discovery of the tiny creature, which the cook had kept living in a glass of salt water, they'd gotten used to his exclamations, but toward evening they saw him leave the galley and come up on deck, and the look on his face alone gave those who saw him a chill. His face was covered in red patches. He must have had them over his whole body, because he was walking gingerly with his legs spread wide and his arms held away from his body, as though the slightest rubbing was causing him excruciating pain. When they saw him, the other sailors were terrified to think that he'd prepared their midday meal with these same, inflamed hands. The captain arrived, noiselessly, in his slippers. For a brief moment he looked at the man from whom everyone was shrinking, then nonchalantly took him by the hand. Without a word, but with remarkable care, he led him across the deck as far as the mainmast hatchway, and the two of them went down into the steerage.

The rest of the crew began a hot debate. The ones who thought they knew the most said the cook's rash was a symptom of the severest form of smallpox. Upon which, the others hastened to add that, in the wake of the latest scientific discoveries, there was no more smallpox, and besides, in order to enlist as a member of the crew, they'd been required to have, among other certificates, proof of vaccination against smallpox.

All the incidents of a sea voyage only make a strong impression when you recount them one after the other. Up until the ray, they'd left the crew somewhat unconcerned. But now they began to reflect seriously on everything they'd seen since they left Madeira. They had a real sense that something, or someone, was pulling the deck of the ship out from under their feet. And now, in the silence of the forecastle, they started to think about the strange feeling of hopelessness that the ray had stirred up from the depths. They reflected on how melancholy it was to have seen colors they were incapable of naming. And they remembered, fearfully, having held between their hands the heart that had been ripped out of the shark, and how it was still so alive, it forced their hands to open.

All this had been no more than a source of distraction and amazement. As already said, if the order had been given to attack the monster, they would have jumped into the whaleboat with joy. And they hadn't hesitated, far from it, to eat the fresh flesh of the shark; but now that they could get a full view of the phenomena they'd witnessed, they were afraid of finding in them a sort of lesson they were incapable of comprehending.

It seemed like it was all being clearly enunciated and a voice greater than any they'd known up until now was speaking, using shapes and colors and smells instead of words. And this hadn't been understood so clearly right away. Rather, it had been weighed down with dread and mystery, before they could manage to make any sense of it. It was Baléchat who tried to explain the matter, the way he'd tried to explain their vomiting. In fact, now that they were breathing the fainter exhalations, whose traces still lingered in the folds of their undershirts, they realized it was simply a floral smell like one you'd inhale in a meadow on dry land. You could almost say it was the smell of a prairie at the bottom of the sea, mixed with the smell of salt air. And yet, just when you had these comforting images in mind, you were stricken with terror at the thought of being saturated with the smell to the point where you'd be obliged to inhale chlorine so as not to die of it.

At this point there was, above all, that other thought, the one stirred by the memory of the wind's open fists pounding and echoing off the islands. It really seemed you were brushing—on every side and on the surface of your skin—against mysterious things for which you had only two, little, ridiculous words, words to which no one attached any importance: Hell and Heaven.

No one knew why, but Baléchat spoke vaguely of the fall of the angels, and while he was talking, he tried with his hands and his outstretched arms to imitate the heavy flapping of a monster being cast into the depths. And from this, it was very easy for each of them to recognize that the leading seaman was evoking their memory of the spectacle of the gigantic ray.

The clearest thing of all was that there was now a symptom, and this was of much graver importance because it had started to manifest itself in the body and flesh of their fellow crewman. Even if the cook's disease wasn't smallpox, it was a disease, and all things considered, they might have preferred it to be smallpox. For smallpox they had remedies. But, as long as this one remained mysterious, they could only resort to mysterious remedies.

And even if they'd known for certain what disease he had, the remedy was uncertain and still to be found.

They ended up being jealous of the amazing vitality that had made the shark's heart leap between their hands. The jeers Marchais and Hervéou hurled at the severed beast came back into their throats. Now they had a great reverence for life.

It was at this point that the captain came up from the steerage, summoned Monsieur Gorri, and conferred with him privately. The captain left, and Gorri came back to the forecastle to announce that the cook had simply been poisoned. He'd admitted to having taken the bird of flames back from the naturalist. He'd left it to hang, like a woodcock, and had made a feast of it the night before.

Nevertheless, there were still some notes of anxiety in Monsieur Gorri's laugh.

IV

Captain's Journal

THE DIMENSIONS of the ship are as follows: length 32 meters, breadth 7.2 meters, draught 4.2 meters.

A slightly bigger boat would have been desirable, but the means we had at our disposal constrained us to stay within these limits. Besides, we consoled ourselves with the thought that, thanks to these modest dimensions, we'd be able to make way more easily through drift ice and to venture into shallow coves. Also, since we're going to be obliged for the most part to navigate without charts, a shallow draught should allow us to spot the seabed before it might put us in any danger.

Here in summary are the specific features of *L'Indien*: the ship is built entirely of oak, except for the planking of the bilges, which is of elm, and of the deck, which is of pitch pine. All the pieces involved in the boat's construction have been made from samples three times stronger than those required by the Véritas inspection bureau for an ordinary vessel of this tonnage. I had a direct hand in this; I made sure myself of the quality of the materials and I closely followed their performance in the tests for resilience. At the level of the waterline, in order to withstand shocks and pressure, the ship is reinforced with sturdy transverse beams. The bow is a massive assemblage of tightly joined wood, and the stem, tapered in order to be able to bear the impact of the swells of the Southern Ocean, is encased in bronze. On the advice of Merlin, this was reinforced at Madeira with some heavy, V-shaped iron fittings. An armored band, eight centimeters thick, protects the hull at the waterline from the wear and tear of the waves.

I want to be able to bear the onslaught of every kind of glory.

So far, the contours of the stern have proved to be well chosen for the sort of sailing I intend to do. I want to be able to vary my speed in the midst of mysteries. There's no need to rush. A layer of insulation, two centimeters thick, lines the wall planking in all of the cabins, and I hope it will be effective during times of extreme cold.

For my own part, I know this isn't so much a voyage of exploration as it is a new way of life. We have to do everything we can to improve our chances.

The vessel is rigged as a three-masted schooner, with lower and upper topsails.

I realized, and I was able to make the people who supported me in this enterprise understand, that the latest discoveries of the age and the advances of science couldn't provide us with any tool that would be particularly valuable to us from here on in. Nevertheless, the ship carries a radio station. But we won't be using it. It's not part of our mission to stay in touch with the world in upheaval. It's pointless to count on that world bringing us aid or assistance. On the contrary, we alone will be able to bring aid and comfort to ourselves. And we certainly won't do it telegraphically.

We're leaving so we won't be turned into beasts. The idea that we could transmit the exaltation of space and light by means of a radiotelegraph set is quite ridiculous.

In fact, this apparatus is kept safely inside crates, in a nook that otherwise contains only a shelf on which I've lined up the complete works of Monsieur de Buffon.

For a while it was debated whether to equip the ship with a one hundred and twenty-five horsepower engine. But, aside from the fact that we would have had to purchase it second-hand, it was obvious that it wouldn't have enough power for the vessel. The steam would have been supplied by two new multi-tubular boilers. The advantages of two boilers of this type—though gained at the expense of sturdiness—over one ordinary boiler would be the rapid build-up of pressure, the minimal consumption of coal, and the option of running only one at a time. But these advantages would be greatly outweighed by the necessity of supplying them with fresh water. My point of view prevailed. Relying on the wind affords me greater freedom. I don't want to be dependent on coal yards, which would force me to set foot in civilized countries.

To begin with we should fill our sails with resentment and bitter longings.

When we're at the far end of the world, it would be wrong if technical requirements subjected us again to the horror of our birthplaces.

We have an excellent windlass supplied by the firm of Moffre in

Nantes. It's been of great importance to me that the sleeping quarters should be as comfortable as possible. There are two meters of headroom throughout, and, no small matter, each of the officers has his own cabin. The forecastle, a little confined for the moment, can easily grow in size once certain storage compartments begin to be emptied out. Then it will become quite spacious. Each crew member has his own little "cabin" to sleep in, a sort of Breton bed with sliding panels, which affords him a bit of privacy. The flexible wooden bedsprings, made of slats, are the same for the crew as they are for the officers. So are the mattresses stuffed with kapok, a substance of inestimable value for expeditions like ours, because it never absorbs humidity and still provides excellent cushioning. The laboratory on deck was set up with meticulous care and the greatest ingenuity. Last but not least, we were able to stow a hundred and seventy tons of provisions and other materials in the hold.

Our unavoidably hasty departure didn't allow us to do enough sea trials. We had to leave, so we left. But while the hull is perfect and the ship handles remarkably well in heavy weather, her sails are poorly balanced. They don't enable us to maneuver when we're close-hauled. I've realized that we make hardly any progress when we're tacking upwind.

This is why, at the latitude of the island of Fernando-Noranla, I gave *La Demoiselle* the freedom to set her own course. She makes better headway than we do, even though her characteristics are the same as *L'Indien's*. I set the Bay of Good Success in the Strait of Le Maire as our rallying point. I could have told her to wait for me at Punta-Arenas, but from now on I'm going to do my utmost not to land at any spot where we might risk encountering anything whatsoever that could remind us of places inhabited by ordinary men.

Aside from the usual fittings, we've brought all the gear necessary for the special conditions in which we intend to navigate. We've laid in enough provisions to last for five years and they've been chosen with the utmost care. The scientific equipment, though limited, is of excellent quality. Besides surgical tools, I consider only microscopes and a telescope of importance. The navigational instruments come from a previous expedition mounted under my supervision in 1924.

I'm particularly grateful to the two Naval officers, Messieurs Larreguy and Jaurena, who didn't hesitate to place themselves under the authority of a civilian, despite the opposition of their superiors. Larreguy and Jaurena have been among my ship's officers from the very start. Even more than the hope that sustains me, the mere gaze of these two men has bolstered my confidence. As well, Monsieur Trocelier, a graduate in engineering from the École Centrale, has given up an outstanding position to join us.

The different tasks that make up our program have been divided between the ship's officers in the following way:

Monsieur Larreguy. Astronomical observations. Hydrography. Study of currents and tides. Salt water chemistry. Planetary gravity.

Monsieur Jaurena. Meteorology. Planetary magnetism. Atmospheric electricity.

Monsieur Trocelier. Upkeep of scientific apparatus. Assistance to sundry observations. Geology. Glaciology. Study of volcanoes.

Monsieur Hour. Zoology and Botany.

I myself am the expedition doctor and will look after everything to do with bacteriology. It was just as easy to recruit the members of the crew. They were selected as follows:

Baléchat, leading seaman; Gorri, "the Red," boatswain; Marchais, seaman; Hervéou, seaman; Archigard, seaman; Roland, deckhand; Paumolle, deckhand; Bernard, deckhand; Libois, deckhand; Brodier, deckhand; Braibant, master carpenter; Jacquier, carpenter's assistant; Noël Guinard, storekeeper; Quéréjéta, ship's cook.

It would be hard to find a better crew than this, more energetic, more devoted, braver, tougher, or more resourceful. Braibant, Archigard, Paumolle, and Noël Guinard have already served under my command. Notably, they accompanied me on an expedition I made to Sala y Gomez in 1920.

An excellent spirit reigns among these men; they aspire only to do their best. They'll never hesitate to go beyond the call of duty, cheerfully and with enthusiasm. I don't mean in times of danger—it would be an insult to raise any doubt in that regard—but even when it comes to jobs that don't pertain to their trade and can often be repulsive. The stated purpose of our expedition is to explore the Western part of Graham Land and to carry out studies in Zoology, Botany, Geology, Paleontology, Bacteriology, Hydrography, Oceanography, Meteorology, planetary Magnetism, atmospheric Electricity, and Gravity. Our probable landing point in Antarctica is at the southwestern extremity of the South Shetlands, Deception Island, where we'll set the chronometers. The mission will spend only two or three days there. We're in no way an Antarctic mission, and our ships haven't been built to hold up to the pressures of overwintering in ice fields. We'll go as far as the open sea will allow us, and during the summer months we'll have to do the best we can to dodge the icebergs. Naturally, during these months, we should travel as far south as we can, to try to get sight of the uncharted territories. But we'll have to take extreme care not to let ourselves get trapped in the icepack. We could neither withstand that imprisonment nor escape it.

Besides, our purpose isn't only to go as far south as possible, but also to explore the smallest bay and smallest inlet of every desert island that can be found between the 66th parallel and the Tropic of Cancer. I'm deliberately giving vague indications; if we can make our way farther south than the 66th parallel, we'll go there; but we have as much work to do above the Antarctic Circle as we do below it. A multitude of tiny islets in the region broadly circumscribed by Chatham Island to the east, Rap Island to the north, Mas à Fiera and the Chilean coast to the west, and Danca Island to the south (or as far as we can go): these are roughly the regions where we intend to work. We'll plot our positions and draw up our charts in conjunction with the men and equipment on *La Demoiselle*.

We have a strange need to find the smallest bit of rock lost in the most desolate stretch of ocean. Aside from this, it isn't the right time, and what's more, it isn't possible for me to talk about my expectations, even in a succinct fashion.

We're absolutely cut off from the rest of the world, free of constraints of time and money.

Because we've brought enough provisions to last for five years, we can't set a date when anyone should have reason to worry about us if we haven't sent any news before then. Nor is it possible for us to map out a preliminary route of any kind where there'd be a likelihood of meeting up with us.

Obviously, we could leave a cairn on Deception Island, but it would serve absolutely no purpose, since it's only starting from there that our adventures will begin.

In any case I'm in complete agreement with Messieurs Larreguy and Jaurena that from now on we should sever all relations and ties with the civilized world. I was fully aware of the implications of leaving the radio station in its crates. Monsieur Trocelier should check, every once in a while, to make sure that this station is operational. When we were departing from Madeira, I shared my perspective with him. I'm not yet fully convinced that he understood me. For the time being, he's obeying me without question. I hope, before we reach the South Shetlands, that I'll have the time to explain, or he'll have the time to comprehend.

Such rare good luck! Our goal is everywhere. What we're seeking will constantly try to hide and flee from us, or it may loom up in front of us without warning and throw us into disarray by its sudden proximity. These are the circumstances in which I'll be drawing up maps and collecting specimens and the results of observations: a sort of catalogue.

If I've decided to fulfill the mission I've been entrusted with, it's because, outside the official terms in which it was laid out, I secretly share the anxiety that had gripped the modern world during the few years preceding my departure. The fact that I have no way of reconnecting with the inhabited world won't make me much different from the common run of men who are living on dry land at the very moment when I'm out on the open sea.

I no longer have any interest in living under the conditions this era allows. To call for help would do nothing more than send us back into the hopeless situation of the rest of the living. I've organized our route so that we have the unknown before us. And the greatest risk we can run is death. In other words, we don't run any risk. To make it known we're in distress, to ask for help, would serve only to return us to that dead-end situation in which all men in the inhabited universe find themselves living.

It isn't possible that life can be only what we've experienced up until now. In spite of our scientific era and the advances we've made, it's undeniable that we're dying of boredom, of distress, and of poverty. I'm talking about a poverty of spirit and a poverty of spectacle.

I'm not a philosopher: I suffer from boredom like everyone else. The vision of my fellow citizens simply arouses in me a feeling of scorn, so unbearable because of the isolation it instantaneously provokes. Other people feel scorn for the rest of humanity, of which I'm a part, and they're just as isolated as I am. If I'm incapable of helping myself, I can't see what help I could get from the inhabited lands. This is why I'm very politely leaving the radio station alone. It would only serve in an awkward way to revive conversations that, even if they've been conducted cleverly up until now, have never been able to rescue any man from his solitude.

I've accepted a certain amount of danger, hoping, thanks to it, to find the greater share of the joys that every man expects. This is more or less the gist of the conversation I had with Monsieur Trocelier. As we head farther south, this is the conversation I'll try to revive if he speaks to me about the radio station again.

Yesterday, on the other hand, I had a long conversation with Monsieur Larreguy.

Larreguy is the sort of man I like. He's twenty-five years old, tall, and tanned. Since he first went to sea, he's let his beard grow, and it's curly and dark. He's a Basque (like his shipmate Jaurena, incidentally) and it was he who brought aboard the cook, Quéréjéta, who's also Basque. I'll talk about him later.

I was touched from the very start by the enthusiasm of Larreguy and Jaurena and I resolved to let them know this at the first opportunity. The only time I was in their company before we embarked, at the office of the Ministry of War, they gave me a strong sense of enthusiasm and security. This wasn't because they were particularly outstanding. On the contrary, I had the impression that I greatly intimidated them, and Larreguy, with the few words he addressed to me at the time, seemed to be stammering like a fool. I don't know what it was in the color of their eyes, in the creases around their mouths, that told me not only of the loneliness of these men, but also of the ease with which they could greet the unknown. Because that's precisely the word. What I'm searching for is the unknown. I don't really care about bringing back new classifications in zoological, geological, botanical, or scientific fields of any kind. Everything we already know along these lines is of no avail as a possible remedy.

For us to return to our home port without having discovered anything unknown would mean we were dying, more certainly than in a shipwreck. This was the same expectation I could see in Larreguy and Jaurena, not in any unusual aspect of their personalities, but in their characters as a whole, and notably in the way they dealt with everyday matters.

I'm passing over all the official, military rigmarole the two of them had to, and were able to, dispense with. I imagine that the attraction, alone, of adventures as part of a small crew (handling a small ship always fills real sailors with enthusiasm) would have been enough to get them to engage in the spirited rebellion that has set them free. But it was in more tangible signs that I could see their motivation. Despite their age, and even though they participated keenly in everyday activities, what I mean to say, and what made them suitable for the goals I'm pursuing, is that they were like extraordinarily red-hot iron blades that instantly evaporate all the water from the basin they're plunged into. I saw them (I experienced this before our final departure, in the last home port, where we spent a week), I saw them hurl themselves with a passion toward everything that could be an excuse for ardor and euphoria. I tried to see if they would succeed in finding, in some of those flights, the vast source of nourishment very man demands. Each time, as I stated so clearly just above, I saw them turn the excuse for ardor and euphoria into steam, and right afterward I found them black and cold and indifferent, like the iron blade you've just plunged into a basin of water. And of course, a short while later, I saw them regain their ruddy glow and sparkle with new desires. But the episode would be repeated over and over, and by the end of the week, I took on board two iron men who were white-hot and unimpaired.

Unimpaired, but a bit lost. I sense that the terror of being perpetually duped by these desperate experiments is starting to take root deep within themselves.

Monsieur Jaurena, who's a little younger than Monsieur Larreguy, seems to appreciate his friend greatly and to follow his lead. I might have talked with Jaurena more than a hundred times already. But I've understood that if I were to have an important conversation with him, it would only matter to him once its importance was confirmed by Larreguy. I have no interest in running the risk of making myself a subject of discussion for anyone, let alone for these two, to whom I've accorded the little bit of respect I can still have for humans. (Here I'm making myself sound superior to what I am in reality. This is always the case when someone writes about himself. In reality I have great respect for these two young men. I have great respect for Noël Guinard. I have great respect for the sailors who've already accompanied me to Sala y Gomez. And I know, alas, I'm not immune to pity. I'll talk about Quéréjéta later.)

Of course, I've had occasion to talk with Larreguy every day since we set sail. But never intimately, always concerning matters of duty. Or in the evening while we're smoking our pipes in the officers' mess. But then his companion would always be there. In this kind of conversation it's important for me not to be drawn into controversies in which young men usually side against those they view as elders. I'm fifty-four and no doubt

I've been through enough skirmishes with joy to appear old for my age. I've been careful, every evening, not to let the conversation turn to subjects other than a warrior's rest and recreation.

I scarcely made this minor observation about the freedom we enjoyed by being out on the open sea, and only after having gathered, from a multitude of intangible signs, that the two friends agreed with me. Of course they agreed. Otherwise it would have been a ridiculous compromise of our expedition's only chance of success. All it would have taken was for Jaurena to have contradicted me, either out of youthfulness or in jest, and it would have become impossible for me to speak, from now on, to the uncorrupted part of the soul that men like my two subordinates conceal within themselves in shame.

It was to this part I wanted to speak. The opportunity arose yesterday evening.

Monsieur Larreguy was up on our little command post. I was well aware we were sailing in a steady wind, as had been the case for the past three weeks, and were holding our course. When I came up to the post, aside from a quiet murmur from the retiring watch who was smoking his last pipe of the day on the forecastle, there was no sound but the drumroll of the sails and the regular squeal of the wheel.

Monsieur Larreguy doesn't smoke. Or very little. He has a pipe, he takes it out of his pocket, he strokes it and fills it with tobacco, but rarely smokes it. Barely once a week.

He was standing with his back to the wind, his feet at right angles to the beam of the ship, happy to be keeping himself upright, hands in his pockets, in that exquisite attitude—that exhilaration of a horseback rider—which fast-running sailing ships always induce in young sailors.

I took my place beside him, in the same position, and I rode horseback with him for a long while in silence. I waited until we'd rocked back and forth for a long while, side by side, moving the same way. He spoke to me first, to let me know he'd had a few reefs put in the sails. Three. This was the right thing to do. I told him so. Then I very cautiously touched on what had made him decide to come on board *L'Indien*, where neither fame nor fortune awaited him.

"That may be so," he answered, "But I'm no angel."

This was odd. But providentially in keeping with what I was hoping for.

"There are," I said, "all sorts of angels."

Then he asked me if I was from Brittany.

I told him:

"No, my mother is from Picardy. This answer," I continued, "must seem baroque to you."

"Less than you think," he said. "I'm more than capable of knowing what you meant."

ME: I said so because I was sure you'd understand.

HIM: I know Picardy pretty well. I haven't been on any long sea voyages yet, except for one world tour, but that was on a battleship. When I got back, I explored Picardy by bicycle. That part of the country appealed to me. I'd seen some of its landscapes through a train window on a previous trip and I knew I'd have to go back there alone.

ME: Alone! There's the word.

HIM: I was there when the apple trees were blossoming. I'm probably going to disappoint you....

ME: I think that will be difficult.

HIM: I can't even tell you the names of the villages I passed through. But one evening I came to a path that ran along the bottom of a narrow valley between two low hills. I had to push my bike because the path was full of mud. There were tracks in the mud from a lot of animals. Especially the huge hoofprint of an ox. I call it an ox. No reasonable person would have called it anything else. Why did I immediately imagine it to be something other than what it was in reality?

(Silence.)

ME: I'm listening. Rest assured I'm listening. I'm not forgetting about the angels. I have the sense we're on the road that leads to them.

HIM: Exactly, monsieur. It would be difficult to tell you, without sounding ridiculous, what sort of animal I imagined from seeing the hoofprint of that ox. Keep in mind, this happened after I got back from the world tour.

ME: A tour during which you claim, nevertheless, monsieur, not to have traveled very much.

HIM: Isn't that how you see it, monsieur?

ME: Not really, I'm just trying to make things clearer. I have a feeling these clarifications will be helpful before long.

HIM: Of course, on the Assyrian tablets there are lots of images of winged bulls, and anyone can recall their lineaments—though I know

I'm using that word like an ignorant sailor—but what I'm getting at underlies the legend that even the youngest schoolboy is familiar with, if he's read Ovid. And before that, there'd already been the winged bull that carried away Europa. The animal I imagined on that night, in that misty hollow in Picardy, after I'd seen the ox's hoofprint, had nothing to do with those mythological or royally barbaric creatures. But, to tell the truth, I should say I didn't see the whole of it.

ME: Which means you didn't *imagine* the whole of it.

HIM: Don't you find it odd to be having this conversation on the bridge?

ME: No, monsieur.

HIM: All right then. That's just it. I didn't imagine the whole form of it. I couldn't imagine the whole of it. But the pieces of what I could imagine burned with such splendor, such magnificence, they filled the part I couldn't see with dazzling reflections. So, while I couldn't see the full extent of the magical beast's shape, I assumed it would be just as interesting as the fragments I could make out.

ME: Equally interesting, or more interesting?

HIM: It was covered by reflections that stopped me from seeing past them, like the sea a little while ago being struck by horizontal rays from the sun.

ME: So, you imagined all this from the hoofprint of the ox?

HIM: Thank you for saying "imagined," without dwelling on what I was imagining. That's exactly how I'd like to be understood. I think it would be laughable for me—I was already fully grown—to dream up something from the hoofprint of an ox. But, as you say, I was imagining. And I don't believe there's anything ridiculous in that.

(*Silence*.)

HIM: May I continue, monsieur?

ME: By all means. I'm keeping quiet only to give you time to picture it again.

HIM: You have a very friendly way of understanding me.

ME: It's natural.

HIM: I don't know if it's natural, but if it is, I couldn't have met many other natural men. Because this is the first time anyone hasn't laughed. Plus, you said something just now that really touched me. It was as if you'd been right inside of me while I was seeing it again. It would be childish to say it was beautiful. Let's use a better word for what I saw in that ravine in Picardy: it was unknown. And now, though I've just seen it for the second time...

ME: Or the thousandth.

HIM: In fact, I have often seen it again, and yes, it continues to be unknown. So that's how, on that night, I suddenly had a new traveling companion. I remember the apple trees were blossoming on both sides of the path. After it wound back and forth a little, it led me to an old fortress made out of black rocks. And that's where I finally spent the night, in the loft, on dry hay. But after my ox's hoofprint had led me to imagine the unknown, everything real that I saw was altered, or reshaped, by my new companion.

ME: That's a common phenomenon in broad, deserted lowlands at night.

HIM: I told you, monsieur, that's how I was able to understand why you answered that your mother came from Picardy.

ME: You don't have to be from Brittany to create angels.

HIM: Before getting to know you, I wouldn't have dared tell you this secret.

ME: You don't know me very well, monsieur.

HIM: No, but I've appreciated your style of command. Should I be telling you so?

ME: Please do. I can never give commands without making a prodigious effort.

HIM: I wouldn't have thought so, monsieur. I apologize again. I'm not in the habit of flattering my superiors.

ME: I'm going to make it easier for you to say what you mean. I'm going to say it for you. You must have felt the orders I was giving were in keeping, most of the time, with your own secret desires.

HIM: Yes.

ME: That's what I aim for, out of consideration.

HIM: But, again, you must have managed to understand the desires of men who are strangers to you. I haven't been your shipmate for long.

ME: What made you want to be my shipmate? I have a rather poor reputation in scientific circles; my expedition to Sala y Gomez has always been considered a joke.

HIM: You've talked about fame and fortune. Usually, people pursue fortune and fame only because they satisfy the heart and the senses. I'm afraid you'll laugh at what I'm going to say now. I'm too young to talk about disillusionment. All the same, I'm telling you very openly: if I believed there were only satisfactions of the heart and the senses, satisfactions you can gain through fame and fortune, I honestly believe, monsieur, I would have packed my bags.

ME: What bags?

HIM: Ah, well, this baggage of body and mind that has me standing here beside you tonight.

ME: You mean you'd have died, to be more precise?

HIM: Exactly, monsieur. The despair that turns men into heroes, if you like, doesn't simply lead to a hotel room and a pistol, or a rope, or poison, or "artificial paradises," but makes them heroes. To do away with myself through heroism, in the eyes of the world and in my own eyes, because I wouldn't have expected anything to come from my actions other than, precisely, the complete disappearance of this baggage of body and mind, which serves no purpose. Maybe you'd have called this cowardice.

ME: No, I don't like hearing that word spoken by men. I don't believe we have the right. I might say impoverishment, destitution.

HIM: So that's how I would have become a hero, through destitution and impoverishment.

ME: Dare I think your decision to set out with me was influenced by that sort of heroism?

HIM: No, monsieur. It wasn't, in any way. The truth is, I still have lots of hopes; in any case, I don't believe that all the joys in this world are included in the catalog we've been taught to rely on. I'm expecting some more. That's what I meant by what I said a minute ago; I'm neither disinterested, nor wise.

ME: Nor ambitious?

HIM: Justifiable ambition.

ME: I'm not insisting, monsieur.

HIM: You can see I'm no angel.

ME: Don't you believe, monsieur, that an angel might take the form of that monstrous fish that surfaced the other day? Everyone took it for a ray, including Monsieur Hour. By the way, did you notice Monsieur Hour went down to his cabin to get his revolver, as if he'd lost his head a little?

HIM: I admit, monsieur, I too lost my head, just a little. It was the first time I'd ever been in the presence of such a monstrous form. What do you think it was, in reality?

ME: Oh, in reality, I'd be very hesitant to put forward a hypothesis. Monsieur Hour claims, through his babbling, that he's had the time to think it over and observe certain features that would connect this fish to the family of rays. I pointed out to him it didn't have a spur on its tail, and we should count ourselves lucky, because we'd have been in serious trouble if it did have a spur and had decided to start using it like a pick-axe. In reality (but as you'll see, this reality has no more scientific validity than the purest product of the imagination), I believe it's a creature of the middle depths.

HIM: I had a different impression. I thought such a monstrous form of life could only arise from the deepest reaches of the abyss.

ME: That's just the long-standing influence of our Christian education and of sacred texts, monsieur. We've been accustomed since childhood to imagine that monsters can only emerge from the deepest abysses. This new adventure, as unusual as it might be—and I admit I've never seen a creature like it, anywhere—believe me, this isn't the true adventure yet. But, if I have to say not just what this animal might be in reality, but what it is in the imagination; if I can go ahead and do with it what you've done with your ox's hoofprint, then I can tell you it's on the basis of forms like this that I picture those angels, the ones we haven't stopped talking about this whole time.

HIM: It's something I'd never thought about. I was stunned when a creature appeared that was so different from anything we're accustomed to seeing. I admit, for a moment or two, I was really concerned for the ship. We were making good headway, and I was anxious our stem would run up between its wings.

ME: Yes, just as you say, even in your nautical parlance: that creature could very well be the image of some preacher discoursing about the angels. At all times, mankind... I'm embarrassed every time I say "mankind," it makes me sound like an old Rousseau; but no, not at all, it's just a convenient word. I'm simply trying to talk about the gloomy, swarming multitudes on the continents we've now left behind. As soon as they feel the shock of seeing the big wings of an angel come into view, these multitudes fear, like you, that they're moving ahead too fast and are going to ram their prow into its feathers.

HIM: I think it would have been a straightforward matter, monsieur. If

Monsieur Hour's opinion really is correct and the creature is a member of the ray family, then it must carry some kind of electrical charge that could be quite dangerous if it were proportional to its size. On top of that, you must have noticed that its skin was as tough as leather, and if you take into account its tonnage, then a hard collision would definitely have made us sink. Angel or fish—if you'll allow me this jest, monsieur—both are quite ticklish, the way I see it. I can easily picture the creature folding back its great wings of skin, like a woodcock that's been shot out of the sky directly overhead, and plunging, completely folded in on itself, toward its beloved abysses. Our fate would have been sealed quickly enough in foam, whirlpools, and wreckage.

ME: I won't deny, like you, I did foresee that eventuality. Even so, everything I'm saying about it is a proof of well-being. It's on this basis that I sustain my appetite for meeting greater angels. In any case, if that eventuality had come to pass, we'd be in the very heart of the mystery today. As it was, while the event was taking place, you and I behaved like normal men in the presence of an angel.

HIM: Would you have wanted for us to have behaved any differently?

ME: Not yet.

HIM: I'm afraid I don't really understand you.

ME: We aren't deeply familiar with each other. But, may I ask you nevertheless to have confidence in me, even if I don't answer your question?

HIM: Of course you may. May I, in turn, ask you to agree to answer certain questions that I'll likely pose to you sooner or later?

ME: I agree completely, monsieur. Did you notice anything in particular about the smell the fish was giving off?

HIM: I did notice that it started to be evident some days before the fish appeared. It must have been following us already...

ME: Unless we'd been sailing over some extraordinary underwater meadows where it had been hiding.

HIM: So you'd allow for the possibility that the smell of the animal might not be its own. I assumed where its wings, or more exactly, its fins joined its body, it must have had some of those scent glands you find in certain aquatic mammals.

ME: It's not a mammal.

HIM: A bird or a fish then.

ME: A fish in the form of a bird. And this is what enables us, in our imagination, to have it plunge just as easily into the abysses of the sky as into the abysses of the sea.

HIM: Your theory of the scented meadow...

ME: What I mean by an underwater scented meadow is its feeding ground. The one where it lives and eats. Where it likes to live... Its May meadow, if you like.

HIM: This way of looking at things leaves me slightly puzzled. Of course, it's highly plausible. I'm even amazed I hadn't thought of it myself. It's a more rational explanation of why that strange smell showed up long before the animal itself appeared. But, from an imaginative point of view, it reduces its importance. It would have been much more dramatic if we'd been escorted by that invisible monster for a number of days. Of course, I know you could say it would have betrayed its presence by some eddies, or by some huge ripples thudding against the hull. Even so, I was quite taken by the idea that we'd drawn it to us, that it had accompanied us for a long time, passing through the abysses we were sailing over, before it showed itself to us.

(*Silence.*)

HIM: All things considered, if the idea of the underwater meadow reduces the grandeur of the monster, it lets us conceive of a parallel order of grandeur, in which the monster isn't an exception, but something normal. This has wonderfully rich implications.

ME: I didn't interrupt you, so that you could realize the implications on your own. And you've met my expectations very nicely: you've discovered exactly what I wanted you to find out for yourself. But didn't you notice anything particularly unusual about the smell? I know it was extremely nauseating, although I have the impression that, to begin with, it was quite pleasant and refined.

HIM: Like everybody else, I blocked my nose and mouth with my handkerchief and stared. I admit it was the smell that terrified me most of all.

ME: To begin with, wasn't it like the slightly sweet scent of meadows of narcissi in flower?

HIM: At the start, even when it was still delicate and faint, and you could mistakenly imagine you were walking through spring meadows, I did notice that sickening sweetness in the smell, which eventually became unbearable.

ME: You didn't notice that it acted on you in a physiological way, that it triggered a mechanical reflex, an impulse?

HIM: Well, yes, I did. It was exactly like that. My body rejected it *a priori*.

ME: Would you allow me, monsieur, to talk about the results of my own observations of that smell?

HIM: Please do, monsieur.

ME: Even if it might be...frightening? I mean, if it might be partly related to why I asked earlier for some moments of silence?

HIM: I believe that you and I understand each other quite well, and from now on you should feel entitled to frighten me when necessary.

ME: Have you fought in a war?

HIM: In this most recent one, I fought on land in Belgium and I survived Dunkerque.

ME: I hope that will do. It was at the start of the summer, wasn't it?

HIM: Yes, monsieur.

ME: I imagine there were a lot of corpses lying out in the sun?

HIM: More than anyone could have wanted.

ME: Doesn't that remind you of anything?

HIM: I suppose it does.

ME: Let's have done with the sentimentality that stands in the way of speaking plainly about things that are considered disgusting, but affect everybody, nonetheless. Haven't you noticed that the smell of corpses makes itself known first (when you don't know yet that it's corpses you're dealing with) by a sugary smell similar to that of narcissi? A sort of syrup, with a stickiness that revolts you as soon as you realize where it's coming from.

HIM: I can see you've gone farther than the rest of us in your observations of the phenomenon.

ME: Do you mean in my observation of corpses?

HIM: I wouldn't have dared say so. I would have considered it disrespectful. What I mean is, you've found exceptional reasons to dread the fish.

ME: Or reasons to hope.

HIM: I count myself more and more lucky to be part of the expedition you're leading, monsieur.

ME: Sometimes it's a lot easier to clarify a conversation that can't help but be ambiguous . . . especially when it concerns something mysterious and when it involves, like ours, a whole series of thrusts and parries (two well-behaved men always have to resort to these); what I mean to say is that it's easier to clarify this sort of conversation through casual banter, or through free associations, as painters say. Do you know how they used to treat what we call internal hemorrhages in days gone by? The doctor would simply suck the wound with his mouth; he'd draw the blood in and spit it out, mechanically. Of course, we're inclined to ridicule this crude, breath-driven pump, but this method does involve direct contact between the mouth of the rescuer and the wound of the injured person. There's great natural virtue in this and, in a way, it's a divine imitation of the healer Hanuman, the Monkey-God.

HIM: Did this method produce good results?

ME: No more than our present-day methods. Its only advantage was that it joined together two separate branches of the truth.

After this we remained silent for a minute. Then I took a short step forward and ended the parallel rocking motion with which we'd both been riding the ship. Bidding Larreguy a good evening, I went down to my cabin.

I've just seen Quéréjéta. I'd a bed set up for him below, outside the infirmary, in a corner of the storeroom. He told me the truth: he did eat the yellow bird. I'd been deeply concerned when his illness started. Like everyone else when they first saw him, I thought he'd had an attack of smallpox, even though the initial symptoms were quite unlike what you observe with that disease. But since I'm ready to embrace all possible manifestations of the unknown, I've spent two days thinking that I shouldn't put absolute faith in my existing knowledge, and that the cook's sickness might be something I'm seeing for the first time. And it is. It has no connection with the smallpox family and it's certainly not contagious. Unless its contagiousness is governed by a completely unknown rhythm, because, since I sent the sick man to bed down below, I've visited him every evening, and while I've had to touch every part of his body in order to do a thorough examination, I haven't noticed any rash breaking out on my skin, even though I'm intentionally not disinfecting myself.

The truth is exactly what he'd told me: he was sensually drawn to the yellow bird and, having spirited it away from the taxidermy lab, he ate it, after letting it, as he put it, hang a little, like a woodcock. I questioned Monsieur Hour to find out if, in the meantime, he might have treated the bird with a solution to preserve it. I asked this because of certain things Quéréjéta said. He told me that, in spite of the heat and the weather, the bird seemed to be impervious to rot. Monsieur Hour assured me he hadn't used any chemical treatment, as he too had been struck by the rock-hard toughness of the flesh, which he could feel through the feathers. What's more, he added, for him it was simply a matter of making the drawing and painting it with watercolors. Which is why, after a day or two, a few feathers would have sufficed to indicate the colors, once he'd done the preliminary sketch. And so, he'd planned purely and simply to throw the carcass into the sea as soon as it started to putrefy.

Since I pointed out to him that he'd acted somewhat casually as a naturalist, and that it might have been a good idea to make a closer examination of the characteristics of this creature, with which neither he nor I was familiar, he assured me that, on the contrary, he knew it very well: it was a tropical Roller. He assured me that, otherwise, he wouldn't have omitted to carefully preserve and identify a specimen he would have viewed as remarkable, or as a discovery.

I asked him if he'd already heard of cases of poisoning amongst those who might have eaten the flesh of that bird in the past. He told me yes, indeed, this had been reported many times, notably among escaped prisoners from Guyana who, lost at sea, had been obliged to use this bird for sustenance. However, as far as he knew, no case had been fatal, and he couldn't tell me if the symptoms of this poisoning were the same as what Quéréjéta had been presenting.

There's no doubt about it: Quéréjéta's body is covered in burns. And on certain parts of his body that I've treated as if they'd been burned, I've obtained clearly observable signs of improvement.

Without question, the sick man is suffering from cutaneous asphyxiation, as if he'd been pulled out of a fiery blaze. Some of his wounds opened up after they began to weep clear fluid and now they're scarred.

Fortunately, it hasn't taken me long to heal the burned patches that appeared at the level of his shoulders and neck.

A particularly odd feature of the illness is that Quéréjéta's face has stayed completely unharmed. It's at the level of his belly and his hips that the patches are the most severe and closely spaced.

From the moment I'm faced with an unknown disease, for which I have to invent the cure, I can't foresee anything about how the illness will progress. Nevertheless, the sick man is calmer. And this evening, after I'd applied his dressings, I was able to communicate with him for a minute or two. During this short conversation, there were even a few hints of a smile. To begin with, when I tried to make him understand how ridiculous it had been to want to prepare a Roller like a woodcock, Quéréjéta had answered with a few words in Basque that meant nothing to me. He began smiling as he translated them into French. They meant, simply: *Everything fills your gut.* I remarked that, for the first time in the seafaring world, a cook was complaining that he didn't have enough to eat. I told him that, in my view, when it came to things to eat, he was, so to speak, at the source. Quéréjéta then talked about the color of the bird, and I gathered it was this color that had attracted him.

When I asked him what the creature tasted like, if it really was good, he answered that it had no taste. But, he added a number of times, it was very good. I understood that, in his mind, it was always about the color. I said: "But you didn't eat the color, did you? The color is in the feathers. Didn't you remove the feathers? The flesh isn't the same color as the feathers, is it? Are you really talking about the color?"

It really was the color. He repeated it to me many times, and since I looked surprised, he started to smile again. With his bandaged hand he made a little motion as if he were signaling that it would be hard to make me understand. At the same time, he repeated the words *argain* and *arrutza garay*.

I questioned Monsieur Jaurena about these words. *Argain* means tall rock, and *arrutza garay* almost the same, as *arrutza* is a rocky place, and *garay*, a height. It's quite possible that Quéréjéta has a bit of delirium, which would be perfectly consistent with the condition he's in.

I must note, however, that the yellow bird—let's call it the tropical Roller to make Monsieur Hour happy—was dashed onto our deck by squalls out of the west twelve days after we'd lost sight of the island of Santiago. During those twelve days we'd sailed due south without interruption and had crossed the equator. When the bird dropped down onto the deck there was no land, in any direction, less than ten thousand kilometers away, except for Santiago, which we'd left far behind to the north. I don't mean to suggest anything, one way or another, by saying this.

After I left Quéréjéta, I went to have a few words with my old friend Noël Guinard. He was sitting under a petrol lamp reading an old manual of Nautical Instructions. He finds this manual very poetic. I said to him:

"All right then, come up to the wardroom, I'll loan you some books." He answered that, between the lines, the ones he possessed and was already reading contained everything he needed. Before we parted he raised his heavy brows and, looking at me over his iron spectacles, said: "It may well be that this time we'll go further than Sala y Gomez."

Monsieur Larreguy maintains that *argain* means sun.

V

Ship's Log

Recorded by Messieurs Larreguy and Jaurena

2 OCTOBER — All day long we've been sailing in light breezes coming out of the east-southeast and the southeast. We've caught a large number of invertebrates, such as different kinds of jellyfish, a small shark, and even some novel species. For a while, in some crosscurrents, I observed a huge, cylindrical mollusk, pale blue in color, at least one meter long and ten centimeters thick, which passed behind the ship.

Monsieur Hour thought it had to be a sea cucumber.

5 October — At 9:00 this morning we sighted, in the south-southwest, a schooner sailing north. At 10:00 it crossed our heading, within about two nautical miles, without hoisting its flag. Since yesterday the heat has been oppressive, especially when the wind drops. Today the trade winds, which had already been blowing less steadily for the past three days, died away completely at 18°S and 16°3'S, to give way to erratic breezes from the south and southwest. Rain fell in torrents, sometimes blocking visibility entirely, while a heavy, dark swell ran through the ocean. There were raging blasts of heat. What we've observed of the limits of the trade winds

formally contradicts Horsburgh, who gives 12°N as their average latitude. Nevertheless, it's my firm belief that heading further west, in the hope of sailing longer with the trades, would be of no avail. Besides, it would be more of a disadvantage to hug too close to the African coast.

10 October — We made the most of a period of dead calm, from noon until 3:00, to measure temperatures at great depths. Ten lengths of line, each a hundred meters long, were spliced together on the deck. The number nine thermometrograph was placed in the brass cylinder manufactured by the Toulon compass factory. Inside it, I placed a small vial containing olive oil, to see if it would solidify. A thirty-kilogram lead weight was attached to the end of the line, four or five meters below the cylinder; and a little above this, a thick-walled glass sphere with a hollow interior.

At 1:52 p.m. we started lowering the spliced lines. By 2:48 all ten of them were in the sea. Because they seemed to be drifting a little aft, I sent a dinghy to tow the ship in that direction, and soon the whole line was descending vertically. At 3:24 we began hauling it back up. We needed the whole crew to lend a hand. The lead weight wasn't back on board until 5:12. It hadn't touched bottom. The pressure of the upper layers of seawater had compressed the cylinder to the point where it was completely flattened. The brass scale of the thermometrograph had been crushed between the instrument's walls. Blown to bits, the tube had vanished, as had the vial of oil. The glass globe came back intact; not one drop of water had seeped into its interior. It had, nonetheless, been subjected to one hundred and fifty atmospheres of pressure.

I greatly regret that this experiment wasn't more successful. We'd mounted it with the utmost care, and it ought to have yielded the true temperature of the sea at that depth. It was the flattening of the brass cylinder that most interested the captain. He took it away to his cabin.

We'd already caught one shark yesterday; today we've landed two more, from three to four meters in length. It's hard to describe the joy and the ecstasy that catches like these always inspire in the crew. It's the veritable enchantment of the savage who holds his arch enemy in his hands and prepares to devour him. This spectacle gives an idea of the excess of enjoyment the direst urge for vengeance can add to the basic appetite aroused by nature, in both animals and men under the absolute sway of the passions. Most of our crew members have always enjoyed eating shark meat. The captain himself has a surprising appetite for it. For my part, without prejudice, and although I wouldn't call this flesh particularly bad, I've always found it to have a peculiar taste, which I dislike. I much prefer a good salted meat.

14 October — Winds from the southwest and south on a heavy, violet-colored sea, marbled with long white stripes. Frequent rain squalls accompanied by shadows, fogs, and foam.

We've decided to make as much headway to the west as we can from this point on, in order to be able to tack our way further south.

25 October — For several days the sky has turned an unusual purplish and violet hue at sunset. The clouds passing across this background have been tinged with sparkling green. This luminous effect always arises in the west. There's no longer any dusk. As soon as the sun disappears below the horizon, night falls fast and hard.

31 October — At 2:15 a.m. I was informed that land had been sighted ahead, a little off to port. At daybreak we could clearly make out three sheer rocks around three miles to windward. By 6:22 a.m. we were sailing alongside them and realized that each of them rose about a hundred meters above the water, which was breaking violently against them. They didn't exhibit any sign of vegetation or animal life. The biggest of the rocks is roughly triangular and thirty meters across its base.

3 November — The heat is rapidly decreasing. Now we see the first Antarctic petrel, at 22° latitude south.

Now, the following day, we've crossed the Tropic of Capricorn. The sky and atmosphere have lost that hazy, whitish cast that prevails in the equatorial regions and they've regained the crystalline, azure purity that imparts to the horizon the clear and sharp lines typical of the South in fair weather.

At 27° S the first albatross appears. The Antarctic and brown petrels have become common. We're gradually lowering our smaller sails to lighten the load on the rigging and prepare ourselves for the rude shocks of the southern oceans.

The weather is superb and the sea is very fair. Carried along by a gentle breeze out of the east-northeast, we've sailed to the supposed position of the island of Saxemburg. At 8:30 in the evening we're in the precise location Horsburgh assigned to this island in 1809. We find nothing here, not even a hint of any form of natural life, no bird, wood, or plant floating on the surface of the sea. Even so, we should have been able to make out a low-lying land mass at a distance of two miles during the day, and at six to seven miles during the night, which was very clear.

9 November — Petrels have become numerous. The sailors have caught a dozen with their lines. This bird is elegant in appearance and behaves much like a pigeon.

11 November — In general, we've had fairly smooth sailing, although we've often had to contend with heavy swells, squalls, contrary winds, and intense heat. However, we've now reached 30° south latitude, and these vast seas of the southern hemisphere are subject to atrocious weather, above all in November. After blowing briskly out the west for quite some time, on the 11th the wind suddenly veered to the south and strengthened. There were a few drops of rain. The sea is starting to run very high and the ship is rolling heavily. We've been forced to heave to.

The gale was of short duration, but the wind continues to blow strongly and the sea is still rough.

13 November — Fair weather.

14 November — Fair weather. At 9:30 in the evening we're in the exact position assigned to Saxemburg by Galloway. No sign of land comes into view. We have to conclude that this island is no more present here than it was in the previous location.

It would be interesting to look into what could have given rise to the absurd stories told by Lords and Galloway concerning the existence of this island. But this could only be accomplished by inspecting their logs.

15 November (*Entry written in the hand of Monsieur Gorri, boatswain.*)

— I've had my share of experience. Once I see something, I'm sure of it. It was twelve midnight. I was part of the second watch, and we'd just come up on deck. Baléchat was acting officer of the watch. Archigard and Brodier were with me on the starboard side. Baléchat, Marchais, and Libois were on the port. To begin with, I could clearly hear the sea breaking on a shoreline. Since the last reckoning had put us at 32° south latitude, this sound astonished me. I called out to the seaman, "Archigard, do you hear that?" He answered: "It's land." I know, the day before at 8:00 in the evening, Monsieur Jaurena was concerned about the position of Saxemburg. I said to the seaman: "It's the island that the officer was trying to sight last night." The seaman answered, "I make it five miles to the east." The wind was blowing stiff, straight out of the north. I called out to Baléchat, who was in command of the watch. I could still distinctly hear the waves breaking on a rugged coastline. Now, however, it seemed that the sound was coming from straight ahead. Baléchat did his best to listen closely, but he couldn't hear anything. I summoned deckhand Brodier. The rest of the watch, who could hear us debating, came to see what it was about. Deckhand Libois could hear the sound more distinctly than the rest of us, but he placed the breakers one mile to the east. Deckhand Brodier couldn't hear anything. Seaman Marchais could hear it faintly. Baléchat voiced some doubts about the reality of what we were hearing, but he told us to be at the ready for maneuvers. At that moment the wind, which had been blowing a near gale straight out of the north, suddenly dropped, and all was calm. I heard Archigard cry out. I ran and

I saw it at the same time he did. Barely a mile to port, the land had just loomed up. There was no moon, but a huge amount of starlight had been revealed by the wind, which had just stirred again and cleared the air. We could see the land plainly. I guessed it to be about five kilometers in length because, from where we were looking, it stretched from stem to stern. Now Baléchat and the rest of the watch could see it too. At first the land was completely dark and stood out only against the stars to the east. Then, no doubt because our eyes were adjusting to the darkness, all of us began to see the features of the coast more and more clearly, as though the moon were full. We thought at first we were drifting rapidly toward it, but we soon gathered it was staying at a steady distance. At the base of some sheer cliffs on the south side, we clearly saw a sickle-shaped beach. This was where the ocean rollers, whose roaring all of us could hear now, were breaking. At one point the starlight became so bright we could make out the color of the vegetation at the top of the cliffs and a kind of grove that ringed the sandy beach that the sea was rolling onto. The vertical rocks were black. Against this background you could distinctly see the white surf leaping up. Though we were certain that the calm waters were keeping us securely in place, everything was in readiness to change our tack if the wind happened to shift to an unfavorable quarter. We could distinctly observe, to the southeast beyond the beach, a cape in the shape of a rat's nose, and beyond that the mass of two or three fairly tall mountains. Among these, at one point, some gleams lit up, which appeared to be coming from fires started by the natives. A number of times, birds we couldn't see, but whose flapping wings we could hear perfectly well, wheeled around the masts. One of them must have swooped down into the crow's nest. We could hear it fluttering around up there for a minute or two, beating its wings. At 12:40 a.m. the wind started to blow offshore, but the mainsail continued to luff. We were catching wind with our main royal only. As a rule, this happens when there's an obstacle between the wind and the sails. I went below to alert the captain. I explained what was happening and he didn't seem surprised. When I entered his cabin he was awake and reading; he interrupted himself only long enough to tell me there was no point in waking up the officers, and when I came off the watch I should record the event in the log book and sign the entry. When I came back up on deck I observed that, in the interim, the wind had shifted back to due north and we were making headway, and that absolutely nothing was visible in any direction.

16 November — It was by order of the captain that boatswain Gorri made the foregoing entry, regarding the sighting he made on the night of the 15th. I regret not having been awakened, but I continue to maintain that the island of Saxemburg does not exist at the given coordinates and that it would be best to remove it completely from the charts, as the English have already done. It's possible that boatswain Gorri might have been deceived by clouds lying low on the horizon. This evening we had a gale out of the west-southwest with tremendous seas. During the night the wind shifted to the south and southeast. Now, the next day, the fury of the sea has abated considerably.

COMMENT — During these gales, the barometer hasn't varied. On the contrary, the level of the mercury has remained very high: 28.4, 28.5, and even 28.6.

20 November — Gale out of the southwest, and right afterward a tempest from the south-southwest with rain squalls, heavy gusts, and a horribly rough sea. The waves are prodigiously high. The ship heeled over as far as 33°. The ship is performing well and not taking on any water.

23 November — During the day the weather improves a little. Northwest wind. We seem to be coming back to life. We get some keen enjoyment from a few minutes of rest.

24 November — Gale out of the north. This time the barometer drops to 27.9. The swell, with its deep troughs, is the heaviest and stiffest we've ever experienced. The rolling it causes is exceptionally powerful and jarring. Floating clumps of giant kelp have begun to appear. On account of the length of the nights, from today onward the crew has been divided into three watches, in order to avoid excessive fatigue. We have to be doubly mindful of the sails.

November 29 — Another gale from the north-northwest. This one lasts all night. Now, on the day of the 30, it has turned into the most dreadful kind of tempest. At 11:00 a.m. it's at its peak of violence. The waves, building into mountains, are rising to at least 25 to 30 meters in height. Fortunately, they're breaking only at their crests; otherwise, they would quickly engulf the ship. I've never seen a sea this monstrous. I didn't believe the equilibrium of the waters could be disturbed to this extent. After we'd battened everything down, we were reduced to sailing with the inner jib alone. The ship has performed well, but it's had to do a lot of hard riding. Some huge waves it couldn't avoid must have opened some seams in the hull, because we've begun to take on water for the first time since we embarked.

COMMENTS — The waves we were taking on board were affecting us like a lukewarm bath. The tempest blew with steady and unceasing fury until 6:00 in the evening, when the gusts subsided and the wind set in fair and steady from the northwest and west-northwest for two days. This was good fortune for us. If the sea hadn't calmed down right away, a swell as tremendous as this would have worn us out badly.

1 December — Light and changeable breezes. At 10:30 in the morning, almost calm. We took advantage and lowered the thermometrograph to 500 meters, perfectly vertical, with a 25-kilogram lead. It came back up in good condition, even though the cylinder was filled with water to within 5 centimeters of the rim. When the cylinder was opened there was a distinct burst of air, a faint puff of smoke, and the water inside was bubbling like sparkling wine.

2 December — Heading east-northeast with a weak, north-easterly breeze and a fairly calm sea. At 8:00 a.m. I spot, not far away to the south, a stretch of sea where the waves are noticeably breaking. On closer inspection the object appears to be the top of a rock, or the hull of a ship, rising only one or two meters above the surface. Some sharp, bluish patches make it seem more likely to be a rock. Moreover, a large number of terns, and clouds of ashy storm-petrels, are cavorting around it. To resolve any uncertainty I have us steer directly toward it. I quickly realize that the supposed rocky protrusion is changing its position, and it finally

disappears entirely. I'm now convinced it's a whale of considerable size covered in shells and coral encrustations. It's also the opinion of Horsburgh that immense cetaceans, when sleeping on the ocean's surface, can produce illusions of this kind.

3 December — Fitful breeze out of the southwest, intervals of rain. Two or three heavy squalls of hail.

4 December — High wind out of the south-southwest.

5 December — The winds come steadily out of the east-southeast, the east-northeast, and the northeast, stiff for the most part and accompanied by fair weather. It's frustrating to be obliged to stay close-hauled on a port tack.

8 December (*From this point on, all entries written by the captain*) — During the night the wind blew strongly out of the north with some occasional gusts. Sky overcast and sea choppy. At 1:30 a.m. I'd ordered the main sail lowered. I was sleeping fairly soundly when, at 6:15, I was awakened with a start by some cries of distress and the sounds of a sudden maneuver. Having raced up on deck, wrapped only in my coat, I soon learned that a man had gone overboard. The officer of the watch, Monsieur Jaurena, had already made all the maneuvers required in such a circumstance: he'd thrown two wooden chicken coops into the sea, hove the ship to, and immediately lowered the small dinghy. As I could still make out the red shirt of the unfortunate sailor who was staying afloat above the rolling waves, and since he was only about ten meters away from the ship, I had no doubt he could be saved. My only anxiety was for the dinghy, whose seams had opened in the heat. To stay as close as possible, I

swung the stern around and brought the ship into irons about fifteen or twenty meters downwind from where the man appeared to be afloat. At the same time, the dinghy was getting rapidly closer to him; however, during this interval, which lasted hardly six or eight minutes, he disappeared from sight. I now learned from his shipmates that he didn't know how to swim, and after he'd been able to keep himself afloat for a short while, with the aid of the air in his clothes, one wave had doubtless been enough to send him under. After a half an hour of searching without success, once we were convinced there was no more hope, I ordered the dinghy back on board and we resumed our route, appalled by this accident. The man who'd perished so unluckily was named Jacquier Benoît, twenty-two years old, carpenter's assistant. At the moment when he fell, he was working alongside Archigard to free up a pail that had been caught in the shroud cables. A strong wave caught him there without warning and dragged him out to sea. If he'd been able to hold on for just a few more minutes, he would undoubtedly have been saved. Despite the wind, the high sea, and the danger they were running themselves, Baléchat, Gorri, Roland, and Monsieur Larreguy displayed courage beyond all praise. The dinghy had only just been raised when the wind picked up considerably, and three hours later it was blowing a gale out of the north-northwest with gusts and a high, rolling sea.

In spite of all our care and precautions, the sails, the hull, and most of all the rigging are beginning to feel the effects of these relentless bouts of extreme weather. I've determined on a change of course to the east, in order to reach some part of the archipelago of Tristan da Cunha. I

feel a pressing need to make landfall, and this is the only dry land anywhere in proximity. I don't expect to find many resources on these rocky
islands. But it's urgent that I give the ship and its small crew a rest. There
are hardly any islands in the seas of Guinea, even though, right up until
the present day, the maps have been strewn forever with illusory lands:
clouds glimpsed on the horizon and taken for islands or reefs by sailors.
I've instructed Larreguy and Jaurena to endeavor, in spite of the weather,
to follow the most direct route possible toward Tristan da Cunha. I'm
worried the poor visibility that's been surrounding us for a while might
cause us to miss this essential respite.

COMMENT — In the evening the sky has taken on a sinister appearance; the bad weather is back.

11 December — From 8:00 in the morning until 10:00 at night we're
obliged to sail with the inner jib alone. The wind is blowing furiously
from the west-southwest along with violent gusts, rain, and hail. It's difficult for us to bear up to the east and we'll probably be driven back into
the waters of the 35° latitude.

The sea, though not as high as the day before, was frightful and much
more dangerous. It was heavier and swept unbroken over the ship. We
couldn't avoid taking on some waves that threatened to sink us every
time. They seeped into every part of the ship. The wind didn't roar, but
howled, during our maneuvers.

14 December — The fury of the wind abated a little on the evening of
the 13th, only to return with renewed force beginning on the morning of
the 14th. This time, though, the temperature is higher, and the gusts are

bringing neither rain nor hail, which makes them easier to bear. Some of the sailors are complaining of stomach pains, and seaman Hervéou fell onto the deck during a heavy roll and injured his head.

19 December — The wind continues to blow a steady gale from the west-southwest, with rough seas and overcast skies. Now, on the evening of the 19th, as though weary of its exertions, the wind suspends its violence and gives the ocean waves a little respite. Finally we can steer a course for Tristan da Cunha. At present the waves are less irregular. They have the appearance of so many connected hillsides in motion, divided by so many valleys, and our ship glides peacefully over them. A truly majestic sight, of which the most skillful pen could convey only a faint impression.

20 December — A new tempest out of the north-northwest, more violent than any of the previous ones, accompanied as well by a leaden sky and continuous rain. The night was frightful and utterly dark. Because I'm steering now on the latitude of Tristan da Cunha and dreading that we might hit upon the island unexpectedly due to an unforeseen current, or an error of our timepieces (which is quite possible after such a long period at sea), I'm choosing to follow a zigzag course while keeping close to this parallel. The ship has labored heavily on some of these tacks, especially on the port side.

21 December — At 6:00 a.m. I set our heading east-southeast. At 7:30 Monsieur Larreguy, on watch, saw the first mass of giant kelp float alongside, and from this moment onward they passed by in great numbers up until 4:00 in the afternoon, when they completely stopped. This kelp, along with the albatrosses that have surrounded us in multitudes, are the

sole indications we have of the proximity of Tristan da Cunha, because we have yet to sight any land at all. However, since we've corrected our course according to measurements of latitude taken yesterday, it's likely that at 6:00 in the morning today we were no more than fifty kilometers north of the archipelago. If there had been no current, or if it had been flowing south in keeping with the wind, we'd have made landfall precisely on Tristan. In any case, with such awful weather and such a heavy sky, it's not surprising we haven't sighted anything. Even during the clearest moments, our horizon extends for only one mile.

25 December — We catch an albatross that weighs 6 kilos and has a wingspan of 1.8 meters. For my dinner I eat some of this "sooty" bird, whose flesh I find good, even better than the petrel's, which I'd already found palatable.

27 December — At 3:00 a.m. the tempest was at the height of its intensity. Monstrously high seas and waves that have become veritable mountains again are mercilessly pounding our poor ship. At the moment, twenty-five centimeters of rain are falling in six hours. The water is seeping into the back of my cabin and leaving all my books, maps, linens, etc., soaked and in a dismal state that will make them hard to preserve.

29 December — Although it's still fierce, the wind is becoming more manageable. We can hoist the topsails, which have been kept furled for so long. Also, we sight a giant petrel.

30 December — Finally we can breathe more easily, and despite the big swell that continues to roll, we're sailing more steadily.

31 December — We were sailing with a fresh following breeze out of

the northwest, on a fairly smooth sea, heading east by south, and I'd given the order to keep a close watch for the approach of land. At 1:00 in the afternoon, from the top-royal spars, deckhand Brodier sighted the coastline about fifty kilometers to the southeast. By around 2:30 we could see the island from the deck. It appeared to be a regular cone, mantled in snow, which rose gradually, very distinct, above the waters. But it was separated from the horizon by masses of fog that made it look as though it was suspended in the air. The sounding lead now measured a hundred and fifty meters, down to a bed of coarse white sand.

We drew in closer to get a better look at the land, and from what we could see, it was beyond any doubt that Tristan da Cunha lay directly before us.

At 6:00 in the morning the following day, the island was still a short distance away to the northeast; we could perfectly make out the smooth, basalt cliffs that plunged vertically into the sea and the waves crashing furiously against them. All day long I steered to the south-southeast to make a wide berth around the reefs that are shown near this island on the charts. At 2:00 in the afternoon on the same day, we were within sight of Inaccessible Island, which lies 32 kilometers from Tristan. We continued to skirt a short distance from its forbidding cliffs, where there was no possibility of landing. Everything we could see looked exactly like a sheer mountain peak looming over the sea. An exceptionally violent backwash lashed against the rocks, sending spume to a prodigious height. We didn't see a single bird or the slightest trace of vegetation. As the coastline of Inaccessible Island is known to plunge steeply, I steered in such a way that we ran along less than a hundred meters from shore. The height of the basalt cliff was so imposing, you felt oppressed when you were facing it directly, as if you were inside a well. At no point could I tell if the cliffs held any nests, and on the entire coastline we sailed past, I couldn't make out any ravine or fault in the cliff walls that would have made it possible to scale them. On the plateau these cliffs lie beneath sat a gigantic, bluish cloud, whose folds hung down, motionless, all along the precipice. When we came out from the lee of these rocks we sighted, twenty kilometers to the south, Rossignol Island, encircled with reefs. The sea was crashing so thunderously against them, we could hear it roaring. Under reduced sail, I endeavored to skirt the round mass of Tristan, to try to reach its north-western part, the only accessible one, where Falmouth Bay is situated.

At 6:00 in the evening, after continuing to rear up as huge pinnacles of vertical rock, the endless basalt cliffs that surround Tristan da Cunha gave way to a gentler slope. We passed within a mile of a sandy indentation that I identified as Flinders Cove. At last, I could steer toward the sandy beaches of Falmouth Bay.

A short-lived gale out of the north nevertheless obliged us to spend the night partly tacking, partly hove to, trying to keep ourselves six or seven miles out from the entrance to the bay, in a position from which we could easily pass inside at daybreak. But the wind from the west shifted south-west, and even south, during the night. Besides, at daybreak, I was disappointed to realize we were south of the cape of Falmouth. In ten hours the current had carried us at least fifteen kilometers to the east. Toward noon, the wind shifted east, and we took advantage to tack west and get ourselves back to the entrance to the bay. From noon until 4:00 the sea was calm. We found ourselves directly in front of the huge belt of gigantic kelp that grow in the waters around the island. On either side of us, heavy rollers were breaking against the ring of cliffs, whose two hook-shaped promontories we could make out to port and starboard. Ahead of us the forest of kelp absorbed the impact of the surf. We pulled one of these vegetal cables out of the water; it had the diameter of a barrel and seemed to have grown to a length of three hundred meters. At 6:00, helped along by a light breeze out of the northwest, we set our course for the far end of Falmouth Bay. At 7:00 I felt fortunate to be able to drop anchor, fully protected, in 8 meters of sandy bottom.

The recent storms have tested us in the extreme. The whole crew is suffering from stomach pains and terrible headaches. During the uninterrupted tempests that have dogged us since the 30th parallel, it's been impossible to give any respite whatsoever to the men. On certain days, the sea appeared so monstrous, it shook everyone's courage and composure. Most of the time we navigated like complete automatons. Two-thirds of our maneuvers were executed by instinct, almost without orders. My own legs are swollen up to the knees. For the time being, it's impossible for me to get the least bit of rest, even lying down. I intend to have a little tent set up onshore, in which we'll be able, I hope, to rest and revive.

As I write this note, darkness has prevented us from determining if there are any inhabitants left at Falmouth Bay. What I was able to observe with the spyglass at 4:00 in the afternoon gave me no hope there could be any other humans here besides ourselves. The four or five cabins I saw, sheltered up against the first cliffs and the reddish slopes at the head of the bay, about four hundred meters from where we're anchored, appeared incredibly dilapidated. In spite of the noise of our maneuvering, and the navigation lights I've ordered to be lit, nothing on shore has indicated that our arrival has been noticed by any human being. A few minutes ago I had the ship's bell rung a dozen times, but there was no sign that anyone heard. Just now Baléchat played the accordion. We've heard neither footsteps, nor a hail, from the beach. According to the last reports, there were a hundred and twelve inhabitants settled together in the little encampment of Falmouth Bay.

Our anchorage is perfectly suited for the season. The bay is very well sheltered from the northwesterlies, the only winds we need fear in these waters in December. The bottom is white sand, and I intend first thing tomorrow to have a second anchor slung to the shore, which is only fifteen meters away. With her two anchors secured, *L'Indien* can withstand any kind of foul weather we can expect here.

Quéréjéta has recovered and will be able to resume his duties starting tomorrow. He still has scars, all over his body, which exactly resemble burns. But, as soon as he was completely healed, I noticed that changes were taking place on his face, which up until then had been unaffected. When he was questioned repeatedly to find out if these changes were a symptom of his illness, he answered each time that he wasn't suffering at all and he felt just as sprightly as he had before his adventure.

Besides, if there had been any remaining doubts about his recovery, his appetite, his good mood and his renewed vigor were enough to dispel them. Nevertheless, I state here for the record that there are two strange and contradictory phenomena going on in Quéréjéta's face. It used to be angular, lean, and dark, like a true Basque. Now, two sorts of phenomena are transforming it. The first one is rounding out its shape. His chin, which was pointed and bony, has already disappeared in the fleshiness. Thinking this could be an effect of the fat he put on during his inactivity, I carefully pressed on his cheeks and came to the realization that the fullness was caused by an enlargement of his cheekbones and his jawbones. It was as though the bones of his cheeks and jaw had begun to grow again. Now he has an almost perfectly round face. His olive-brown complexion used to be rather dark. Now his skin has become the color of copper, and every day you can see it acquiring more and more golden highlights. His hair, which used to be black and curly, is becoming flatter and more flowing. I wouldn't be surprised if it turned white or light blond. I've already seen signs of this in the roots.

The second phenomenon that has altered the face of Quéréjéta is as follows: his eyes have become smaller—elongated and almond-shaped. When his lids are wide open and he's at rest, which happens sometimes when I'm sitting next to him under the pretext of taking his pulse, his gaze has a strange quality of depth and calm, which it didn't have before. His mouth, which has inevitably widened with the expansion of his jawbones, has become imperturbably expressionless. I know of no other face that conveys such a great impression of serenity and peace.

It occurs to me that we forgot to celebrate Christmas.

V

Noël Guinard's Adventure

> If you would send me your pipes with all their little
> trinkims, I would put them in order myself and play
> some melancholy tunes, well suited, might I say,
> to my wretched position as a prisoner.
> —letter from Auld Reekie

O N THE MORNING of January 1st, the sun leapt into the sky. It
was the height of springtime in the southern hemisphere. Far to
the south, bad weather must have been lingering inside a thick
bank of violet clouds, where lightning sometimes bristled and flashes of
copper silently quivered. There was a light northwesterly breeze. Along
with the salt smell of the vast reaches it had traversed, it carried gentle
waves of warmth. To the north the sea was barely forming whitecaps. The
waters of Falmouth Bay were as smooth as a lake. Along the high basalt
cliffs, morning cries began as the slabs of rock warmed up. Rollers breaking against the two points that protected the bay exploded into foam,
which was instantly lit with iridescence by the sun.

Noël Guinard knocked on the captain's door. Stepping inside, he took a good look around before asking: "Are you alone?" "As you see," the captain said. Guinard shut the door and came and sat on the edge of the berth. "How are you?" he asked. "As you see," the captain said. Guinard rubbed his chin for a while. "I'd like to go ashore. What do you say to that?" "We'd all like to," said the captain. "I plan to set up a forge over there," said Guinard. "Have you already been up on deck?" asked the captain. "No," said Guinard. "You don't know if the island's inhabited?" "The Instructions say it is." "So the Instructions say, with four thousand kilometers of ocean in every direction." "I want to go ashore. As I said, I'd like to pitch a tent there and build a forge." "You'll have to sign requisitions for the material." "Already done," said Guinard. "All right, then, you can go."

Noël Guinard went ashore in the rowboat that was carrying Monsieur Larreguy, deckhand Libois, and master carpenter Braibant. These three were assigned to investigate the handful of dwellings visible at the foot of the reddish wall at the head of the bay.

Past the sands on the beach, they saw traces of a path that looked like it had been trod on only a short time before, and it led them to the first four cabins. They were built of old planks and all their doors were open. The men went inside. There were no signs of recent habitation; all the nails that had been driven into the walls had been prized out; empty, rusted tin cans were scattered across the floor.

They carried on walking toward the foot of the cliff, where they saw fifteen more wooden houses. But all of them were equally bare inside.

Except for one, where it looked like a cloth curtain was moving in a window. They knocked on the door, but no one answered. After a moment, Monsieur Larreguy gave it a push with his foot, and it opened. The room was small, four meters by five. In the middle, a table with some kitchen utensils; in particular, a huge, blackened frying pan. Libois ran his finger around the inside and found a little fresh grease. On the corner of the hearth there was a pile of dried brown kelp covered in old, ripped open tin cans. On a shelf next to the window, Monsieur Larreguy found two dust-covered books: *Don Quixote* in Spanish, and Milton's *Paradise Lost* in English. As a craftsman, Braibant admired the heavy table, which appeared to have been fashioned out of flotsam from shipwrecks. But it was Noël Guinard who made the most intriguing find.

Hanging behind the door was a huge, woven basket made from strands of dried seaweed. Out of this gourd-shaped receptacle, Guinard pulled a skirt and a blouse. At the bottom of the basket, there was also one of those broad, long-handled knives with a blade five centimeters wide and twelve long, slightly curved and finely ground, the kind whalers use. There was much debate about the women's clothes; they didn't seem very old. What's more, they seemed to have been worn recently. There was no sign of any other clothing in the room, nor any trace whatsoever of fresh food or provisions. However, Libois, and then Braibant, confirmed again that there was a thin layer of fresh grease covering the whole surface of the frying pan. The fireplace, which they examined closely, contained only white, powdery ash and no remnant of coals. The rest of the room was bare, except for a sort of crude chest in which they found an enormous quantity of rusty nails, whose curvature indicated that they'd been prized out with tongs.

Monsieur Larreguy decided they would go and report these findings to the captain, and Noël Guinard parted very courteously from the rest of the group.

Right behind the house, the cliffs rose vertically for a good hundred meters, but a crevice separating two large, fractured slabs of the rock face made it possible to climb to the top. Noël Guinard began ascending through the scree. He was a short, lean man who got winded quickly. Every ten or twenty meters, he stopped to catch his breath, and each time he looked around he saw no signs of vegetation or any nests. When he finally arrived at the cliff top and hoisted himself up onto the plateau, the scene in front of him was magnificent. First, there was a sort of low ledge, two to three hundred meters wide, between the upper edge of the cliff and the bottom terrace of an extraordinary massif, entirely volcanic from base to peak. Past the lower slopes, and almost directly overhead, Noël Guinard could see the triangular, snow-covered summit of the Tristan volcano vanishing into the upper reaches.

When the sun had risen on the eastern horizon at 7:00 in the morning, it had abated all the winds. A profound calm prevailed at these heights. The mountain was surrounded by perfect silence on every side. You could no longer even hear the crash of the ocean rollers that thundered incessantly, even though, when they broke with violence inside the basalt caverns under the surface, they sometimes exploded like cannon shots. When he leaned out a little over the abyss, Guinard could see the foam boiling far below. But no sound rose up to meet him.

An extraordinary expanse of sea stretched into the distance to dissolve into a sky of the same color and, without a trace of transition, reappeared high overhead as the backdrop to the sharp peaks of the volcano. Lit by the sun, the lava of the mountainside was beginning to show its greenish iridescence, and it took Guinard quite a while to realize what he'd taken to be the tangled branches of a forest were actually nothing more than heaps of blackish serpentine rock, which had slid down from the upper terraces. He proceeded across the narrow, basalt plateau and could see, here and there, possible starting points for an ascent.

But before attempting to continue his adventure in that direction, he took a leisurely stroll to explore this level plateau toward the west. Except for some gravel, which was rounded like beach pebbles and must have been shaped by the high winds, Guinard was walking across a pure table of basalt, so level he could start to keep his hands behind his back. Completely at ease, he headed west.

It was almost noon by the time he'd made his way far enough to sight the opposite side of the island. As he now realized, the island of Tristan was almost conical, like the skirt of a spinning Spanish dancer. On the far side, the huge folds in the rocks reached all the way down into the sea. They were like the pleats in a dancer's flared skirts, which fill out when she whirls. But here, the dancer's feet stood in water four thousand meters deep, and the laces of her skirts were tied around a volcano instead of a woman's waist.

The basalt shelf hung over a dark abyss. Down below, more than a hundred folds of rock, enclosing more than a hundred dark chasms, rose directly out of the sea. Noël Guinard came forward, right to the edge of the precipice. At the bottom, he could see the sea foam boiling, luminous. He still kept his hands behind his back. He spent a long time looking at these rocky ridges. The sun had already started to pass around to the other side of the island when he, too, decided to turn on his heel and slowly retrace his steps. He examined the side of the mountain more attentively and gradually took stock of the possible lines of ascent. He stopped for a while in front of each of them and studied the footholds, one after the other, as far as his eyes could see. Then he found himself back at his point of departure, at the summit of the rockslide above the cabins. The afternoon wind was beginning to blow onto this side of the island. This was a light breeze out of the west, remarkably persistent despite its weakness. It blew against the bare slopes of the mountain. As it passed over the stones, it stirred up a variety of sounds, some of them as supple as if they'd been aroused from tree branches. These sounds were accompanied by a little clicking, caused by the heat of the sun as it warmed the slabs of schist.

If you closed your eyes, you could imagine wind passing over dry palm trees. But when you looked at the mountain, you were immediately struck by the bareness of the rock. Noël Guinard closed his eyes several times and reopened them to look around at the forbidding desert that this breeze, unobstructed for thousands of kilometers, was caressing. Several times he thought he heard a repeated note, like bird song, to his left. He cautiously approached the spot it was coming from. He could see that that it was issuing from a tiny crack in the rocks—over which the wind was passing—that acted like the mouthpiece of a terra cotta bird call, the kind people use to lure thrushes. Further along, on his right, a low-pitched rumbling began to build, intermittent at first, then sustained. When it was at its height it seemed to be bellowing from a throat lined with velvet. The rumbling was entirely controlled by the variations in the wind and followed all its rhythms. As he walked forward, he realized it was produced by a slightly larger indentation, in the form of a conch shell, through which it seemed as though the wind was calling out to the eastern sea. Higher up, the rock being struck directly by the breeze was chirping like a flock of skylarks; and at even higher elevations, where you could sight the triangle of snow at the volcano's peak, the wind must have been singing a much more fulsome song. At times, it blew muffled roars, like massive organ pipes, all the way down to Noël Guinard.

What surprised him was that the wind didn't stir up any dust. For eons, breezes had streamed onto the most secluded ledges with such regularity, the basalt rock faces were worn smooth and shiny. Not a single plant, not the least vestige of wild grass, or moss, or lichen, revealed the wind's movement. Guinard searched systematically all around to confirm this absolute emptiness. Nothing indicated the eye of the wind. Its presence was revealed only by the various songs it sang as it streamed across the stones; by its coolness as it passed over Guinard's body; and by the salt smell it carried. This clarity made the desert even more beautiful.

Noël Guinard stayed perfectly motionless for a long time, focusing his gaze inch by inch, until he'd made sure of the absolute stillness of the world around him. Although the ocean was traversed by the great, green swell of the South Atlantic, from this high vantage point it too looked completely motionless, and the sky, perfectly uniform in color from the rim of the horizon to the summit of the volcano, rounded out the utter stillness of the world. For a long while, without shifting position, Guinard's eyes searched slowly all around him for the tiniest hint of movement. Gradually, he became absolutely convinced that everything was fixed solidly in place.

Now, slowly, he began to move.

Up until now he'd studied his surroundings without stirring, content to shift only his eyes from one side to the other. But once he was convinced that nothing was moving and nothing could begin to move, he decided to turn his head to fix the positions, first, of the sky, and then, of the sea. Then, having studied the rock wall in front of him, he moved slowly toward it, chose the few footholds that would enable him to begin the climb, carefully positioned his feet and hands, and began to ascend with remarkable slowness.

The basalt rock wall wasn't completely vertical. A little oblique, its surface was broken enough for Noël Guinard to be able to make his way up without much effort or particular skill. He proceeded with the same bourgeois complacency he'd maintained during the whole of his morning stroll along the top of the cliffs. Most of the time, he made sure of his grip with only a few toes and fingers, and during the climb he would pause to gaze calmly right and left, sometimes even to daydream.

He gradually climbed five hundred meters of the rock face, taking his time, gazing leisurely, not only right and left, but also above, contemplating the emptiness during pauses he seemed to regret having to end. In this fashion he reached a first ledge, barely a few meters wide. As soon as he'd gained a foothold, he carefully brushed off his knees and the front of his wool jersey.

From here he could gaze down past the edge of the cliffs. He saw a large, moon-like crescent of the foam that dashed relentlessly against the sheer coastline of Tristan. Finally, in this surging foam, he thought he perceived hints of movement within the world that surrounded him. But while he was frowning with disappointment at this observation, he perceived that, from this height, the foam itself, which leapt up constantly along the base of the cliffs, appeared every bit as motionless as the snow on the volcano. Now he regained his serenity, and his eyes narrowed like those of a cat that has settled on a warm hearth. From up here even the long swell of rollers that besieged Tristan and broke against its coastline appeared to be motionless, made up of several concentric circles of dark green water, frozen for good on the surface of the sea. When he was completely convinced of this, Guinard closed his eyes and enjoyed a long moment of satisfaction. Like he'd done earlier, at the base of the cliffs he was about to scale, he began to move extremely slowly. And now, at this higher elevation, he exaggerated the placid quality of his movements. He remained for a long time with his nose right up against the rock face he was going to continue to climb, before he raised one arm over his head and slowly got a grip on a tiny handhold. He leaned against it and pulled, lifting his compact, lightweight body. He carefully positioned his toes on a rough patch of black serpentine where the sun was lighting up furtive flashes, and slowly started to scale the second wall.

This wall, which must have been more than a hundred meters high, was on a more comfortable incline than the first one. Starting a few dozen meters above the ledge, it even allowed Guinard to release his hands at times. He took advantage of this to sit down, then to stretch out on his back. In this way, he was juxtaposed directly with the sky. Against his back, a basalt wall; against his belly, a wall of sky. With a rapid glance he made sure that the rocks couldn't encroach on his view of the sky, either to the right or to the left, and now he breathed a long sigh of contentment and began to gaze with infinite joy at the utmost emptiness that can exist on earth.

By now, he was so accustomed to the moaning of the breeze, he no longer heard it. It was due to a minuscule alteration in the brightness of the sky that he realized the sun had begun to descend toward the west. He got up. As the slope allowed, he calmly held his hands behind his back and completed his upward climb.

He now observed that the high point he'd reached was separated from the main mass of the mountain by a narrow crevasse. It was so steep and narrow, its floor must have been in perpetual shadow ever since the island first formed. Standing with his hands behind his back, he began to look for ways to get down into this chasm. It appeared to be very difficult. Even the location of the floor, hidden in shadow, was hard to make out. The wall across from him, on which the afternoon sun was striking, was perfectly vertical and completely smooth. But the high point he was standing on was a crescent-shaped ridge. It disappeared to the right and left behind shoulders of rock where there might be possibilities for continuing his ascent. The scene you saw from here was striking in its grandeur; when he lifted his eyes suddenly amid this limitless expanse, Noël Guinard's gaze met nothing but the undifferentiated green of sky and sea. Inaccessible Island and Nightingale Island were hidden to the southwest by the mass of the volcano itself, and in the direction in which Noël Guinard could look out over the sea, he could see nothing but sea and sky. So he sat down calmly on the ground and pulled a little mirror and a pair of scissors from one of his pants pockets.

He made himself comfortable, placed the mirror between his knees, and after turning his head right and left to make sure the wind had really stopped, he cautiously began to trim his beard. It was extremely long and bushy. He began by combing it with his fingers. Next, because the mirror was too small to reflect his whole face, he moved his head around in every direction to work out the shape he was going to give his beard. He started to trim it straight across the bottom, carefully putting the strands into his pocket. He studied how he looked with this new beard. Then he rounded the corners and, to finish, he ran all the way up his cheeks with his scissors. He was pulling on the corners of his mouth to make the hairs stand up. Each time he cut some strands, he put them carefully into his pocket, and when he let one or two of them slip to the ground, he gathered them up with care.

When he thought he'd finished, he took the mirror in his hands.

Studying himself from every angle, he knew he had to redo the full curve, combing it repeatedly with his fingers, until it was as perfect as it would have been in the hands of a barber. He blew on his scissors to clean them off, wiped them on the thigh of his pants, and put them back in his pocket. Holding the mirror up from every angle, he gave himself a final inspection, which satisfied him. Then he rolled the mirror up in his handkerchief and put it into a separate pocket of his smock.

The sun was setting; it was still high above the horizon, but soon it would plummet like a stone. You could tell this moment was fast approaching, by barely perceptible trails, violet at first, then blackish, that began to crisscross the sky; they lit up into broad beams, starting from a point on the western horizon, and then shot into the sky like the half-extinguished rays of a huge, black sun.

Noël Guinard, making sure that his scissors and mirror were safely in his pockets, stood up and decided to go and see what possibilities there were for getting past the crevasse that separated him from the main mass of the mountain. For this purpose he took an iron pince-nez from his fob pocket, unfolded it, and placed it on his nose. He began his investigations toward the right, but hadn't yet gone a hundred meters before he realized that, in this direction, the crevasse—which kept getting wider as far as the eye could see—cut off any possible connection with the other side. So he turned back to the left. Shortly after he rounded the bend, he found that, in this direction, on the contrary, the two lips of the vertical walls came closer together and then fused, so he could perfectly well continue his ascent. He refolded his pince-nez and, having stuffed it back into his pants, began to climb a slope that was still quite steep, but on which he could stay upright.

He'd put his hands behind his back again and started to climb at his strolling pace, taking care to look closely all around him, stopping to make miraculous observations of even the smallest handfuls of serpentine debris. As far as the eye could see, without a doubt, there wasn't the slightest sign of vegetation, not even a wisp of grass as fine as a spider's web.

Suddenly, the sun went down. Where it had touched the sea, there was a huge, incandescent patch that shifted rapidly from blue to red, and then to violet, and grew in size. When the violet reached the shores of Tristan da Cunha, it was night.

Overhead, huge, dark beams had joined together just as rapidly. In the heavens, which had suddenly turned pitch-black, the stars lit up, all at once, in every direction.

Noël Guinard had continued climbing very calmly. He paused every ten meters or so to catch his breath. The air was deliciously sharp. There wasn't the least hint of wind. A few minutes earlier, after the sun had set and was casting the last of its colors across the sea, Noël Guinard had observed with a rapid glance that the water was as smooth as a lake for an astonishing distance.

Now it was impossible to tell if he was still walking on real ground. If it weren't for his shortness of breath from the climb, which obliged him to halt from time to time, he could have imagined he was walking across the floor of a narrow, sealed-up room, so profound was the silence on every side.

Each time he stopped, he didn't turn his head right or left. Instead, like a horse that gathers its strength for a second, heavy pull, he stayed still in one spot, catching his breath, and simply lowered his head. In this way he quickly found himself in the shadows, with no glints of reflected light. Even his footsteps made no sound, because he was wearing espadrilles, and the mountain floor, swept clean of any gravel, was as smooth as a board.

Only the air he was inhaling smelled of the open sea.

After a few minutes the slope began to grow steeper. He was obliged to halt more often to catch his breath. At one point he instinctively touched the fob pocket in his pants to check that his pince-nez was secure. Finally, he came to an area where, even with his head lowered, he couldn't avoid seeing—at the level of his chin and in every direction—a part of the starry sky. Ahead of him, despite the dark, he made out the paleness of the snows that crowned the summit of Tristan. Despite those stars, which were starting to crowd around his face, and before he made any further move, he dug into his pants pocket and pulled out a little roll of chewing tobacco. He raised it to his mouth, bit off a wad, and started chewing carefully. When the juice had passed its peak of acridness, he decided to feel around the spot he was in and choose a hollow where he could sit. As soon as he sat down, he saw the night.

It was entirely blanketed with stars, from one rim to the other. Some were the size of peas, others of lead shot, while others looked like clouds of dust. There was no patch bigger than a thumbnail that wasn't filled to overflowing with this luminous dust. During the day, the northerly breeze had cleared the haze so well, the stars were shining now with unimaginable purity. It was impossible to make out where the heavens stopped and the sea began, because the sea, no doubt smooth as a mirror from the farthest horizon all the way to the coast of Tristan, bore the reflections of all the stars. The very mass of the mountain, near, at least, to where Guinard was sitting, started to glimmer with the same sort of reflections firing from the countless facets of serpentine, whose crystals were completely fresh. None of this was earthly. Down below, amid all the stars' reflections, you could barely make out the navigation lights of *L'Indien*.

Nevertheless, Guinard quickly recognized the little red and green sparks that marked the port and starboard sides of the world he'd left behind that morning.

If you hadn't known that a boat was anchored some fifteen hundred meters straight below, it would have been easy to imagine some colored planets down there. But Guinard knew very well they were the lights of the ship. Even so, he kept furiously chewing his tobacco, until he'd reached the state of exaltation a fresh wad never failed to produce in him. Then, gently shutting his eyelids, he narrowed his gaze until he could make the navigation lights migrate nicely into the world of the stars.

From that moment on, he remained so rigid that, before long, the blood started to drain from his fingers and his feet. The extremities of his icy limbs were full of tingling. He kept trying not to move, but soon he no longer wanted to: the tingling had ceased and his limbs were consumed in the frozen cold.

At the same time, his whole torso, and especially the region of his heart, lungs, and belly, was filled with a prodigious heat. A completely bloodred life force, which he felt he was seeing through a sphere of glass, was filling him. He could gradually open his eyes without dreading the intrusive stain of the green and red navigation lights. They had crossed over, for good, into the world of the stars.

He had fully succeeded in making the world around him disappear. He didn't need to move to feel that his burning blood was beginning to flow back toward his hands and his feet. He could feel it sliding, little by little, along all his fingers. It was filling his whole skin with a new life, which went to beat at the extremities farthest from his heart. He succeeded in moving his fingers and toes in a natural and flexible way, and having assured himself of the state of being he'd reached, he took some deep breaths and opened his eyes wide.

The stars closed around him meticulously, surrounding him in an unbroken sphere. The silence was so perfect that, a short time later, he even began to hear them crackling. This started in his eyes with some throbbing, or some sharply pointed shafts, which made the constellations pulse rapidly all together, as if a wind out of the depths had slowly stirred their distant embers. Then, in the total silence, which filled his ears like the finest flour, he started to hear the crackling of distant fires. The biggest stars made muffled, creaking sounds and sometimes emitted a short, crystalline cry in concert with the gold and blue flames they were shooting out. The multitudes of luminous particles scattering in all directions through the night sky were making a hushed sound like the chafing of falling snow. At times, even from these muffled depths, a rustling rose up and grew. It came from a long, golden spray that spanned the sky from north to south in a slow procession of flames. Into its wake, the night sky, reunited again, rained down new stars. While the revolving night was driving its flocks of stars to the zenith and then herding them down to the sea, the song rumbling on one side of the horizon was growing louder with the sonorities of newly risen stars.

Around Guinard there was no sound whatsoever. He was motionless, except for the movement of his jaws as he chewed his wad of tobacco.

The whole time the transshipment of stars from west to east was underway, Guinard remained perfectly still. He attended to all the most subtle variations in the embers' crackling, which was filling the heavens. He had no need to turn his head; the moment a constellation rose in the east, he became aware of it right away, as if it were a beautiful new voice entering a choir. He would hear it take its place amid the overall song of the stars, and the modulation it introduced evolved into a new melody within the general arrangement. Each time a constellation disappeared below the western horizon, a whole section of the overall song went quiet to make room for the rising constellations. Gradually, however, the crackling of this distant concert of sounds diminished, and by the time night itself seemed to have wrapped itself in a milky grey, the song was nothing more than a gentle murmur. Suddenly, everything fell silent. At the same time, the stars faded out all together, and it was day.

Noël Guinard stood up and carefully brushed off the back of his pants. He felt in his pockets for the scissors, the mirror, and the pince-nez. He began to make his way briskly down the slope. When he reached the first plateau, he quickly discovered a rock slide to his left that would be easier to descend than the wall he'd scaled up the evening before. He started down and soon was back on the basalt plateau that overlooked the cliffs. He looked for the fault that led to the cabins, found it, got down to the beach, and from the water's edge hailed the dinghy. It was Libois who came to pick him up. Guinard climbed the ship's ladder. Once on the deck of *L'Indien* again, he joined his hands behind his back. He encountered the captain. "Did that stroll go well?" "Very well," said Noël Guinard.

VII

Tristan

T HEY'D SET UP the forge on the sand beach, near the first cabin. From time to time, the captain was spending the night in the house where they'd discovered some women's clothes.

Monsieur Hour had succeeded in finding some plant specimens. Turning to the right of the beach toward the crevices in the rocks, he'd encountered a miniature fern, a lycopod, and a prickly cordgrass he was thrilled to identify as *spartina drundinacea*. He claimed that, beyond these insurmountable rocks, and inside the hollows of the cliff, which plunged vertically into the sea, he'd seen a contorted tree—completely coiled down to the ground, like a snake—that he believed was a kind of buckthorn (*philica arborea*). He was bubbling over with enthusiasm; he absolutely wanted to take command of the small whaleboat and skirt alongside the rocks, to get himself to the very spot over which this kind of tree stood. Eventually the captain gave the order to man the small dinghy with leading seaman Baléchat and deckhand Paumolle.

Monsieur Trocelier hesitated to join the expedition. He was torn between the desire to identify botanical rarities, and the desire to engage with a few other men in the ascent of the volcano, where he wanted to start his geological and vulcanological studies. The captain brought a swift end to his indecision by advising him to go on the expedition most in keeping with the mission to which he was personally assigned.

Early in the morning, not long after sunrise, Monsieur Hour and Monsieur Trocelier each got underway. Seaman Hervéou, deckhand Roland, and deckhand Brodier were assigned to accompany Trocelier.

Leading seaman Baléchat, having headed out to sea in the small dinghy, quickly rounded the point to the northwest, beyond which the inlet overhung by the twisted tree was supposed to lie. As soon as they'd gotten past, they found themselves in the grip of the wild, pitching rollers crashing nonstop against the cliffs. Despite the windless weather, these rollers—which rose irrepressibly two hundred meters from the shore— grew coming in, and by the time they broke against the black walls of the island they were more than three meters high. Before the men could think of examining the features of the coastline and venturing into the inlet Monsieur Hour had identified, Baléchat shouted out that, for dear life, they'd better pull hard on their oars straight away. All three set to rowing with all their strength to escape a roller that was bearing down on them close to the wall. With fanatical dexterity, Baléchat made the dinghy take the roller full on the bow. When the wave broke against the rock face, they were being hurled stern first at high speed toward the basalt wall, as though they'd smash into it, but the immediate backwash rapidly drew them back out to sea, just as their stern was already brushing against the rock. "Pull hard!" Baléchat yelled, "let's get the hell out of here, men, this is the damnedest mess I've ever seen in my life." They rode overtop of a second roller, then the start of a third, and once past the place where the waves were forming, they found themselves in calm water. Baléchat dropped his oars and let out a long whistle. "Never seen death from that close up," he said. "What happened there?" Hour asked. "Caught in the jaws of a devil of a pair of pincers," said Baléchat.

Paumolle was looking at the breakers, which didn't stop crashing furiously against the wall and sending jets of spray up tens of meters. Now the dinghy was resting perfectly calm. Monsieur Hour, scanning the cliffside, found the location of his tree and pointed it out to the two other men.

"If you want to feel it with your bare hands," said Baléchat, "even though in my opinion it isn't worth the trouble, the best way would be for us to sling you from a rope and lower you down from the summit. By sea, it would be devilishly hard. There's nobody I know who'd be able to bring you in close."

Nevertheless, they went a little farther to the northwest, but still couldn't see any possible landing place. However, the waters they were in now, outside the area where the rollers were forming, were perfectly calm. There was no wind. They returned to the ship, where they explained at length the reasons for their failure. But what they said about the buckthorn was enough to interest Trocelier and the other three men in going to look for similar trees, assuming there were other specimens on the island. If there were none, as a last resort they'd follow Baléchat's advice and sling Monsieur Hour down to his tree from the edge of the cliff.

Larreguy, who'd been meeting on board with the captain that morning, was very pleased Baléchat had returned. They had to take advantage of their stopover at Tristan, and the remarkable calmness of the sea, to go two miles north to drop a sounding line and conduct a new experiment with the thermometrograph. Larreguy gave the order to rig the big dinghy, and at 11:00 in the morning, it was ready to embark. Larreguy had chosen Baléchat and Gorri as his crew, along with Marchais and Archigard.

To avoid Baléchat's misadventure, they headed due west from the island, opposite Falmouth Bay, directly through the big patch of giant brown kelp; they had to struggle for more than an hour to free themselves from this grassy swamp. But they reached calm water without further obstacle. From there they gradually made headway, rowing to the northwest, and toward 2:00 in the afternoon they were in the area for taking soundings and began lowering two thousand meters of line. The thermometrograph, placed fifty meters above the sounding lead, was stabilized as well by two thirty-kilogram weights, enough to hold it in its proper position.

Up until a thousand meters of line, the lead dropped straight down without interruption. At this point it appeared to have touched bottom, and stayed so slack for a minute that it began to coil back under the boat. Finally, some loops of rope floated up. Monsieur Larreguy brought the unwinding to a halt and made a note of the depth. But while he was busy with this, the few meters of rope that were floating in a circle near the prow of the dinghy sank abruptly with a peculiar sucking sound.

Right away the sounding machine drum started to whirl at such high speed, Gorri had to drench it with capfuls of water several times to prevent the hemp rope, which was starting to smoke, from bursting into flames. In astonishment, they observed that the line was pulling down so hard on the prow of the rowboat, it was on the verge of taking on water. At Larreguy's signal, Marchais and Archigard grabbed hold of the oars and prepared to row. Baléchat had drawn his big knife and was poised to cut the line; Larreguy signaled him to wait. Gorri continued to drench the drum with water he was scooping up in his beret. At Larreguy's signal, Marchais and Archigard tried rowing to give a little slack to the line, which was still unreeling at high speed and was coming close to its end. Though they were propelling the rowboat enough to keep up, the line remained incredibly taut, and even began to drag the boat forward.

Larreguy leaned over the gunwale, and as far as he could see, through the limpid depths, the line was no longer perpendicular but stretched out on a steep angle ahead of them. Not speaking a word, and with Baléchat always at the ready to cut the line with his knife, they were towed along for more than half an hour, not in a straight line, but in a big circle that gradually brought them back to their point of departure. The moment the two thousand meters of line were about to have come completely unwound, a shock jarred the rowboat so strongly that Larreguy, standing upright in the bow, came tumbling into the arms of Gorri, who held fast onto the gunwale. The boat was motionless, and the line completely slack, which allowed the bow to rise up again. "One hell of a big fish!" said Baléchat. "I don't know what it is," said Larreguy.

The sea was still placid. Only the big, circular wake described by the rowboat remained visible. They began immediately to pull up the sounding lead. They'd let out the whole two thousand meters. A good thousand meters came up in a completely normal way, then another fifteen hundred. It continued, but they couldn't feel the weight of the leads anymore. Finally, the end of the line emerged. It had been broken off cleanly at about seventeen hundred meters. The fittings and the weights had stayed in the sea. They inspected the break; the hemp there was simply stretched out; however, in a knot stuck to the hemp a little before the break, Gorri found a glob of rubbery white stuff that would fit in your fist and smelled of musk. Larreguy put it carefully aside, and they pulled hard on the oars to get back to the ship before nightfall.

He went directly to the captain to relate the adventure. When he showed him the handful of white rubber they'd removed from near the end of the line, the captain, intrigued, felt the weight of the stuff and sniffed it.

"Ah," he said, "I believe it's him, the old devil." When Larreguy asked him if he knew what it was about, the captain merely sniffed the handful of rubber once or twice more, while repeating: "It's the old devil, monsieur; you're going to find out what the old devil is. I will explain it to you, but for tonight, Monsieur Larreguy, you can go to bed in peace, and leave this little piece of musk with me. I believe you've encountered first-hand one of those old abominations that men aren't accustomed to seeing. I have twenty years of ocean dredging behind me. Rest assured, not everybody gets to hold a rubber ball like the one you had in your pocket.

All the lands we know of, you and I, monsieur," he said, while tapping a simple planisphere mounted on the wall of his cabin, "all this," he said, "America, Asia, Africa, I'll even throw in the little there is of Oceania, all this is nothing more than one big island lost in the midst of oceans four times as vast. We're at the very source. Give orders to have the whaleboat rigged early tomorrow morning."

The following morning at dawn, the captain, choosing the same men who'd been in the whaleboat the day before, set off toward the spot where the line had broken. When they got there, he had them stop rowing and pull in the oars. After a minute the boat came to a standstill, as though it were planted in the sea. The water stretched away around it, without a ripple, as smooth as a mirror. The captain lay on the gunwale at the bow and stayed there looking into the depths. "One hell of a big fish," said Gorri. "One hell of a big fish," said the captain. "How far northwest of the island are we?" "Two miles." He stood back up and dusted his knees. "Men," he said, "we're sitting right above one hell of a deep trench. It looks like there wasn't much chance of touching bottom with your lead."

"Nevertheless," said Larreguy, "it did touch something at twelve hundred meters." And he related the incident where the line had gone slack and floated up. "There's no question you touched something," said the captain, "but it wasn't the sea floor. You touched the old devil." "Sea monster?" said Larreguy, with a slight curl of his lip. "I hope we'll get to witness the spectacle," said the captain, without answering the question directly.

"I hope this is where we'll have our first encounter with the real world," he added. He gave the order to return to the ship.

"Where have you been living for the last while?" he asked Larreguy. "For three months I was in Toulon, in the Saint-Jean-du-Var quarter." "Were you having your meals in an officers' mess?" "Only at midday. In the evenings, the chambermaid made my supper." "I don't know Saint-Jean-du-Var," said the captain, "what's it like?" "Suburban, cheap little villas, gardens with cabbages and lettuces, middle-class pensioners." "Glass balls?" asked the captain. "What's that?" "I'm asking if there were glass balls in the gardens." "It's not the fashion in that part of the country," said Larreguy. "There's enough to look at all around, so you don't need that sort of device for daydreaming." "Goodness," said the captain, "what is there to look at around there?" "Lovely, bronze-colored mountains to the north, monsieur, and a whole patchwork of olive groves, more beautiful and strange than the gardens of Armida." "Goodness," said the captain. "Gardens of Armida, I like that a lot. And," he said, "was the grocery store far away?" Larreguy smiled: "I didn't pay much attention to the grocery store, the chambermaid looked after that, but if you need to know the specific detail, fifty meters from my place there was not only a grocery shop run by a Greek, but a Casino chain store as well." "Perfect," said the captain. "That detail is really worth noting. I like the Casino chain store a lot. Don't imagine I'm wasting my time: suburban gardens, cabbages and lettuce for retirees from the shipyards, a Casino outlet, and even the gardens of Armida, all this makes up, monsieur, the scale by which we're going to be able to gauge exactly the grandeur of the spectacle, if we're lucky enough to be given the chance."

Monsieur Trocelier hadn't yet returned to the ship. But, on the sloping flank of the volcano, they could see a little thread of smoke that looked like it was coming from a campfire.

During the afternoon the captain went ashore and he asked Monsieur Jaurena to accompany him. As they were crossing the beach in the direction of the cabin where they'd found the women's clothes, the captain asked Jaurena if he'd had time to speak with his friend Larreguy. "He's very interested, monsieur," said Jaurena. "I hear you've made it known that we're going to be lucky enough to witness a spectacle." "Not lucky," said the captain, "but fortunate, and good fortune isn't granted to everyone. Besides, I don't know if we'll be granted this good fortune. In any event," he said, "since the start of our voyage we've been favored with portents that seem to suggest we're on the right course." "Scientific discovery?" Jaurena asked. "Sentimental discovery," the captain responded. "Have I neglected to tell you, Monsieur Jaurena, that I'm a sentimentalist?"

"By the way," the captain said, as they were arriving at the cabin, "what's your opinion about Noël Guinard's little discovery? Are you experienced enough to be able to tell much from a woman's blouse?" "Not with precision," said Jaurena, "but if it's a European blouse, I'd be able to tell whether it's up-to-date, or old-fashioned." "Ah, well! You see," said the captain, "science shouldn't overlook anything, and I have the feeling, Monsieur Jaurena, if you've rubbed shoulders with high-fashion designers, you're going to be able to help us clear up this little mystery." He plunged his hand into the gourd-shaped basket and pulled out the blouse and skirt. Jaurena felt their weight and spread them out. "They seem plain," he said, "but they're not bad, really." "All right," said the captain, "picture a woman wearing these in Paris, or on a sunny afternoon on the Canebière in Marseille, for example. "Excellent!" said Jaurena. "She'd breeze right by. She'd be a typist on her way to work at her Insurance Company." "A woman or a girl?" asked the captain. "Your saying typist makes me wonder." "A girl," said Jaurena, "or a petite woman, at any rate." While he was examining the garments from every angle, he instinctively raised them to his nostrils. "Very shrewd," said the captain, "I'm surprised Noël Guinard didn't think of that. What's the perfume?" But Monsieur Jaurena's eyes had opened wide. "It's not a perfume, monsieur, it's an odor. They still smell of sweat."

That evening when darkness fell they kept a close eye on the beach, in case Trocelier's men came down and hailed for the boat. But not long after, red embers from a campfire were seen glimmering on the flank of the volcano.

The expedition party came back the following day a little before noon.

Their news: they'd discovered a freshwater spring. This was especially important because everyone had been concerned about replenishing the ship's water supply, in view of the long crossing, without landings, they still had to make between Tristan da Cunha and Tierra del Fuego. The spring was located in the ravines that wound their way down between the mounds hanging from the western flank of the volcano. As far as Monsieur Trocelier had been able to determine, the waters of the spring, which they'd seen issuing from a point halfway up the mountainside, flowed down in a stream toward the sea. They disappeared by the shore, forming a tiny white sand beach where it might be possible to land. Since Trocelier had already made such a precise chart of the location, the barrels were immediately raised and readied to be placed on land, where they could be caulked and sulfured ahead of time.

The other news Trocelier and his men brought back was also of importance. First, they'd killed two wild pigs on the northern flanks of the volcano. For one thing, these animals were of great zoological interest. They weren't wild boars, they were similar to domesticated pigs, but Monsieur Trocelier claimed they were exceptionally ferocious. The sailors had driven them into a cul-de-sac in one of the ravines, where, even though the beasts had been wounded by several rifle shots, they continued to put up stubborn resistance, to the point where they even wounded deckhand Roland with a deep bite on his calf.

After Monsieur Hour had taken their measurements, performed his autopsy, and recorded the details in his catalog, the pigs were delivered to Quéréjéta to prepare for the crew's meal. Monsieur Trocelier claimed they'd heard, several times during the night, and not far from their encampment, meows as if from a sizable cat. In addition, Trocelier, who'd explored the north, west, and south flanks of the island, had found they were generally covered, though thinly in parts, in a prickly cordgrass that grew in tufts so tangled in several places, it was impossible to penetrate the dense thicket. He'd also found some more accessible specimens of buckthorn. "In certain spots," he said, "it's a tree that reaches five or six meters in height. But it usually bends right down to the ground, no doubt because of the relentless winds, with its trunk coiled against the earth like a snake." For his colleague Monsieur Hour, he'd brought back some branches and roots.

As well, Trocelier believed that certain kinds of vegetation, different from those he'd already collected, must be growing on several tiny beaches on the south side. Through his telescope, from above, he'd observed that these beaches appeared to be covered in green, thick-leaved plants. Trocelier had pushed on all the way to the summit of the volcano, reaching it the evening before. He'd camped all night nearby with his men. This summit consisted of a crater, regular in form, containing a fresh water lake that appeared to be very deep and absolutely pure royal blue in color.

On the same day, from the moment he reached the summit, Trocelier had been able to follow from above the misadventure that befell Larreguy's whaleboat during the sounding expedition. He said that, from his vantage point, he'd been struck at first by the peculiar color of the sea where the boat had stopped to lower the lead.

"Right along all its shores, the water surrounding the island is light yellow in color. Starting a mile out to sea, it turns a shade of green. But very distinctly, in the area where the boat was at rest, the water was an intense shade of blue. From there, all the way around to the west, it kept this same color." He'd noticed, not long after the boat came to a standstill, the water around it had darkened considerably. From the heights, his gaze was falling perpendicularly down to the water.

With the telescope, he'd followed all the movements of the whaleboat while it was being towed by the sounding line, and he confirmed that the speed at which the boat had been swept along appeared, from high up, to be very great. For a long time he'd wondered what force had been able to drag the boat at such a speed, which no oars could possibly have produced.

To be able to camp easily for the night, they'd gone several hundred meters down the mountainside and lit a fire on a small, rocky ledge. They were still overlooking, from far above, the place where the whaleboat had taken the sounding. Toward two in the morning, Monsieur Trocelier, having awakened, noticed their fire had completely died out. He stayed on his feet for a long while to admire the exceptional sparkling of the sky, which was blanketed with stars. It was then, he said, that his attention was caught by a series of phosphorescent flashes. At first he'd assumed it was lightning from a distant storm. Gradually, he realized these flashes were coming from the sea, but they were quite unlike any other marine phosphorescence one usually saw at these latitudes. "In particular," he said, "they weren't continuous, but intermittent, separated by long periods of darkness. They burst exactly the way bolts of lightning burst from inside a cloud, and they lit up considerable stretches of the sea with puffs of purple and sulfur yellow." It was obvious they weren't coming from the surface, but from the depths, and they were extraordinarily intense. Because, although they were abrupt and violent like lightning, and he was seeing them cast their glow over several square kilometers, they nevertheless had the softness of a light emitted far below that was gradually shimmering up to the surface.

After he'd gazed at this spectacle for a while, and because it continued to display a more and more surprising strangeness, he couldn't hold back from waking up seaman Hervéou, who was more familiar with marine life, to ask if he could explain this phenomenon.

Hervéou stood gaping for long while. Then, all he could do was to let out some exclamations that woke up the deckhands. The four men went on looking at this amazing, underwater storm. "It was located," said Monsieur Trocelier, "exactly in the position where the whaleboat had been towed away by the sounding line." On the rest of the surface of the sea there was only an impenetrable darkness and the faded reflection of the stars. But there, in the very place where they'd taken the sounding, the fiery flickering, like the pulsation of a strange, luminous life-form, continued to light up the waters to the rhythm of one flash every couple of minutes.

"At first" said Monsieur Trocelier, "it was an explosion of purple that dazzled you, even though it was coming from deep, dark waters. A second later, a wide stretch of the sea lit up and shivered, all roiled up with red. Then a saffron yellow light spread even further out of sight, and then everything faded, suddenly, the way a fishing net sinks when it's weighted with lead. The spectacle was so incredible, we held our breath during each explosion, and only had time to take a breath or two before the underwater lightning would flash again." This was amply confirmed by Hervéou, Roland, and Brodier. They'd stayed on their feet all night in uninterrupted contemplation of this phenomenon. As dawn approached, they hadn't been able to tell whether the intensity of the underwater illumination had diminished, or if the sun had made it disappear in its continuous blaze.

In addition to this, Monsieur Trocelier had made an excellent start to his geological research. He'd collected more than twenty kilos of different kinds of ore and tested them straightaway in the laboratory. He suspected they must contain copper, sulfur, and maybe even cinnabar, because in the area where he'd gathered the specimens, he'd been severely irritated by mercury vapors. He even claimed it was these vapors that were keeping birds away. Indeed, since they'd arrived at the island, they hadn't seen a single bird, either at sea or on land. He and Monsieur Hour had a heated debate on this subject.

The following morning the captain, who'd decided to go and investigate the watering places they'd discovered, ordered the whaleboat to be fitted out. He selected Jaurena, Baléchat, Archigard, Roland, Paumolle, and Bernard as his crew. He left Larreguy in command of the ship. Before he departed, he arranged for a distribution of tobacco, and fishing line and gear, and ordered those who were staying behind to try and catch as many fish as possible in the course of the day. All the fish they caught were to be submitted first to Monsieur Hour for inspection. He would draw up a catalog, then hand them over to Quéréjéta for cooking.

The whaleboat embarked early in the morning, and they soon lost sight of it behind the rocky outcrops to the north. The weather stayed perfectly calm, and the strokes of the three sailors, driven by Archigard's relentless rhythm, quickly had the boat making steady progress. By noon they'd located the watering place identified by Trocelier. It was in an indentation in the cliff wall, facing directly east. On this side the rollers, which broke so violently on the western shores, were smaller and calmer, making it possible to land. And, in fact, they were able to steer their way onto the little white sand beach with ease.

The quality of the water was excellent. Nevertheless, they filled several bottles for analysis on the ship.

Not only did the beach, where the water fell from a height of several meters, have enough room for the row of sulfured barrels to be lined up safe from any backwash; but also, as a sounding revealed, the coastal shelf dropped precipitously five meters offshore, making it possible to draw the ship in close enough to easily set up a conduit from the spring itself all the way to the ship's reservoir.

These discoveries relieved a great deal of worry. The crew of the whale-boat had their midday meal on the sand beach. While they were eating, their attention was caught by an enormous, white mass the rollers were driving toward the shore. Though this piece of flotsam was being buffeted by a stiff backwash that caused it to surface and then disappear, the seawater kept spraying up around it. At first glance it appeared to be the capsized keel of a large, open boat. However, it was surprisingly white. When it had come closer, and before it disappeared behind the rocks to the south, the captain recognized it was the belly of a dead sperm whale or a humpback. Since there was no foul odor, they could assume the animal had died recently. But the captain made the point that they hadn't seen any whaling ship cruising in the vicinity. After a brief silence, he ordered them to put their meal aside and man the whaleboat to meet up with the floating object.

The corpse, which looked enormous once they came closer, had continued to drift due south. Pushed farther from shore by the current running around a small promontory, it was on its way back out to sea. Nevertheless, they quickly caught up with it, and the captain asked them to circle around two or three times to be able to examine it from every side.

It was a dead sperm whale. In the depths, they could see its head lying upside down with its jaws open. The captain quickly stripped, and when Jaurena asked him what he planned to do, he told him he needed to know what kind of death this sperm whale had suffered. He intended to dive underneath the animal to find out if it had been harpooned. If this were the case, he was sure to catch sight of a wooden shaft, or the burst of a harpoon cannon shell, on the back of the whale, which had submerged at the moment when, dead, it had turned belly up.

The color of the water where they were floating let them think it must be very deep. Monsieur Jaurena, offering to accompany the captain on his dive, was already getting out of his pea jacket. But the captain told him, with a smile, that they mustn't put two officers at risk at once. Archigard, who was burning with impatience, volunteered, got the captain's nod, and stripped bare in an instant. He was the first to dive, the captain followed, and the white shapes of the two men could be seen sinking below the monster. A minute later they resurfaced on the other side and hailed. The whaleboat went around, and they grabbed onto its side. There was no sign of a harpoon or any wound on the back. While he was still in the water, the captain asked the boat to draw in tight against the corpse. From here, the captain and Archigard made several more dives, appearing sometimes at the head, sometimes at the tail. Finally, the captain, coming back to grab the side of the boat, asked the sailors if they'd brought knives. Roland always had a huge one on his belt. The captain asked him to plunge it into the creature, a little above where the corpse broke the surface. Then, using the boat's gunwale and the knife as footholds, the captain climbed onto the floating wreck and began to examine it.

Measuring it with his stride, he estimated it to be about eight meters long, but in this way, he was measuring only the belly of the animal; its total length under the surface had to be at least twice that. The captain scrutinized some wide, red, round marks that scarred the belly. Archigard, who'd stayed in the water, claimed they were the animal's teats, but the captain asked him to dive to try and see if, under the water, the creature didn't have similar marks on its sides or back. When he resurfaced, Archigard said that, in fact, not far down, he'd been able to make out the same kind of round, pink marks. They were the size of dinner plates. Archigard added that he'd seen, near the head, some large, deep, parallel tears, like sword cuts, that were already full of little, flesh-eating fish. The captain told Archigard to climb back into the boat, while he himself, taking hold of the knife that had been embedded in the side of the creature, easily cut out a piece of flesh that bore one of these marks. The sailors maintained they could get enough blubber from the corpse to make a barrelful of oil, but the captain told them they weren't whalers, and that, besides, he considered the flesh of this animal unfit for consumption. Archigard, who'd often had occasion to eat sperm whale, begged for permission to carve off a slice near the tail. But the captain gave the official order not to touch the corpse in any way. He tossed the strip he'd cut, which bore the red mark, into the boat, and, leaving the hulk behind, they returned to the beach at the watering place.

On close examination this red mark looked like it could have been made by an enormous suction cup. While the sailors were smoking their pipes, the captain and Monsieur Jaurena walked back toward the waterfall. Jaurena could no longer hide how intrigued he was by all the effort the captain had made to determine how the animal had died.

"Couldn't some whales, especially where the coastline is steep like this, simply be driven ashore and battered to death against the rocks?" "This one," said the captain, "wasn't battered, and I'm waiting until we're back on the ship safe and sound to tell the men just how it died." Monsieur Jaurena's eyes widened. "You, too, monsieur," the captain said. "I think it would be best if you didn't know any more about it for another few hours." When the sun passed around to the other side of the volcano, they left the beach and reached the ship before sunset.

The captain asked his officers to stay on board for the night and he advised the crew members to do the same. However, he asked those who weren't at full strength, who'd sleep better on land, to make a point of staying in the cabins nearest the shore, where they could easily be hailed. Before the evening meal, the captain summoned the officers to his cabin. He sent especially for Monsieur Trocelier, who was still occupied in the laboratory with his experiments.

When the men came in, the captain was strolling around his cabin. He had Monsieur Larreguy stand next to him. Pointing to the piece he'd cut from the corpse of the whale, he asked them all to examine it carefully. "Take a good look," he said. "I think I'll have to point some things out. What do you make of this, here?" Everyone had heard about the encounter with the whale. "This is what killed the animal," he said, and looked at Monsieur Jaurena. "A disease?" asked Monsieur Hour. "No," said the captain. "It's not a disease. They're wounds. The dead whale we found is young. It didn't have the size or strength of one of those old rogues that have already cruised the Pacific from top to bottom plenty of times. But it was hungry. Are you familiar, Monsieur Hour, with how sperm whales feed?" "Birds and land mammals are more my specialty!" "All right" said the captain, "they feed themselves in a very particular way. Mainly with a sort of squid we suspect lives in the deep ocean trenches. The sperm whale can't dive deeper than a hundred and fifty or two hundred meters. We have to assume the squid it preys on must climb some four or five thousand meters from where it usually lives, all the way to the limit of where the whale can come down to reach it. We even have to consider the possibility that the squid might rise a lot higher, perhaps all the way to fifty meters from the surface. Maybe, at times, it even breaks the surface. I should tell you, I've never seen one. No one has ever seen one." He turned to Larreguy, who'd already raised his hand two or three times to interrupt. "What amazes me is that you're talking about it in the singular," Larreguy said. "You've just spoken of *one* squid. We know very well what a squid is, and without knowing how much the sperm whale needs, I suspect, if squid is what it eats, it must need tons of it. So, I wonder why you're talking about a single squid, when it must be a matter of a whole school of squid." "Please have a look at this object," the captain said, pointing to a zinc basin where he'd placed the slice of whale flesh. "This little trifle is exactly thirty-eight centimeters in diameter. You aren't wrong to imagine that this round, pink mark looks like one left by a sucker. Indeed, it is the mark left by a sucker." There was a moment of silence during which, without shifting position, the whole group of officers leaned over the basin. "You're right," continued the captain, "when you maintain the sperm whale needs to eat tons of squid. It doesn't mean, monsieur, these tons have to come from a school of little squid. They can come from a single squid that weighs several tons." "This is miraculous," said Larreguy. "This is not the last miracle we'll see," said the captain. "It's only the first. We've been warned, and there are two things preparing us. One, that ball of rubbery stuff you found sticking to your hemp sounding line the other day." From his pocket, he pulled out the little piece of rubber Larreguy had given him. "And the other, this sucker."

"I'm not venturing anything here, messieurs, that I don't know for a fact. Others have already had the opportunity, and I too, to study the formless remains of this giant squid. We've found them in the stinking mass of food a sperm whale spews out the moment it's wounded. These remains usually sink to the bottom right away. But I myself was given the chance, over near Sala y Gomez, to examine a segment of a tentacle made entirely of the white, rubbery stuff you see here; the same kind of tentacle that caused these nice, round, pink craters. If you can project, from this segment, the length of the tentacle it was originally a part of, you come up with more than a hundred meters. I leave it to you to imagine the full scale of the creature that could possess tentacles this long".

"A nice present to give to a child," murmured Monsieur Larreguy. "In fact, the most beautiful present you could possibly give," said the captain.

"But please do sit down, messieurs, and allow me to offer you a glass of an exceptional absinthe that has survived two world wars. I've been keeping the bottle for a special occasion."

He took a bottle of 1906 Pernod out of his cupboard, and once they'd mixed the liqueur with a little water, it emitted its renewed fragrance. Each of them felt considerably altered after the first few sips.

"A curious feeling," said Monsieur Hour. "None of you is old enough," said the captain, "to sip striking memories from your glass. In the days when this beverage was common on every café table, you hadn't even begun to nurse. What's going to happen to us, messieurs, or at least, what I hope is going to happen to us, is something like the surprise the absinthe is making you feel in your hearts. It's an admirable old poison, meant for stronger heads than ours. However, I'm convinced that, in the end, it will offer a splendid solution to the impoverishment we've been reduced to little by little, and from which, little by little, the world is going to expire. We might even say this is where we're harvesting the fragrant Lotus.

"I don't believe a single one of you, despite your youth, despite the enthusiasm I see in you, can look upon the life you've led up till now without feelings of disgust. Can you really tell me, Monsieur Hour, that your profession, as fine as it may be, has been rewarding enough to let you contemplate the rest of your eighty years or so of life without fear of boredom?" "Unless," said Monsieur Hour, with a laugh, "I run into the squid." "I don't think it will be particularly vicious with us," said the captain. "Nevertheless, I don't recommend you go and kiss it on the mouth. And I believe," he continued, "neither Monsieur Trocelier, nor Monsieur Jaurena, nor Monsieur Larreguy, will contradict me when I maintain we're perishing of pettiness and deadly boredom.

"It's for these same reasons that men less civilized than we are, but (and I say 'but' intentionally) more innocent than we are, closer to the origins of things, more attuned to sensing the proximity of the great mysteries, have always kept themselves well supplied with monsters.

"Without leaving for foreign countries, and with each of us remaining in his own birthplace, we only have to go back a few hundred years to find Ariosto's orcas, the dragons of the Arthurian legends, and—I'm thinking now about the little book we found in the deserted cabin—Don Quixote's cave of Montesinos. It seems, since then, our reason, more unreasonable than the worst kinds of madness, has led us to live in an arid world where the new breed of monsters has made neither chivalry, nor grandeur—apart from those planes and tanks, gorged on gasoline, that obey the rage of partisan passions—possible. So now, humanity, in its drunken fever, has started carrying on about gestures and words, and in spite of all our goodwill, men like you and me haven't taken long to grow supremely weary of this carrying-on, in which there's no longer any nourishment for these petty dreams of grandeur, if I may say so.

"I believe it's of the greatest importance, gentlemen, that we not be turned into beasts. Our spirit has need of space and light, of fiery skies, and of the exaltation that all of these bestow. Once upon a time, we looked for them in here," he said, taking hold of the bottle of Pernod, "behind this label, and my goodness, it is quite pretty, all in all. But from time to time, nature, which we haven't entirely suppressed, still brings into being some men who are just as true, just as pure as those men in the past who couldn't consume a single ounce of meat unless it was accompanied by all the foods of the spirit. These men will continue to demand the Paradise they naturally believe (and are right to believe) they're entitled to by birth. Damn it! It's plainly true they're right to believe.

"I'll never assume you are what you are, and I am what I am, only so as to squander the time left to us, by living in the way we see life being lived at this moment on the continents we've forsaken."

He stopped to clear his throat and drink. The four men's silence obliged him to continue.

"To spin round and round like tops," he said, "to get excited by political regimes that consist, most of the time, of the most despicable murderers, the most despicable because they set themselves beyond the reach of any punishment and pass laws that give themselves free rein. To exhaust one's curiosity—such a fresh, enticing feeling—on puny objects offered up by the so-called progress of civilization. To circle through the interminable, barren corridors of this strange segment of the earth that consists of the inhabited continents, and most of all, to accept losing touch with the real world: hasn't all this brought you to this arid state, full of sarcasm and disgust? And in this state (I don't know much about your former lives), have you, possibly, concealed your grander aspirations for space and light?"

He was interrupted by Quéréjéta, who came to call them to dinner.

"We'll have to pursue this further," said the captain as he stood up, "and I'd like to have the benefit of your insights. Keep in mind, however, that even in the iciest regions there's always a Swedenborg, and a William Blake, to beat us over the brows with angels until we run out of breath. So, gentlemen," he said, while steering them toward the mess door, "why not try to discover things that are real in the rest of the world? This is what's left for us to do, I believe, before we surrender to despair."

Quéréjéta brought a wonderful dish to the table. At first glance, it filled their eyes with gold and purple magnificence. Then, as soon they'd tasted it, they were so taken aback by its excellence, they summoned the cook to congratulate him and ask how he'd done it. It was a simple matter, he said. After Monsieur Hour had examined the fish the sailors had caught earlier in the day, he'd told the cook to take the firkin to the kitchen. The cook had found himself confronted with rockfish whose colorings were exceptionally intense and pleasing. Right away, purely by association with the colors, he pictured saffron, curry, onion, garlic, parsley, wine (they cried out for him to stop!): everything that could enrich and complement the majestic colors inside the firkin.

Having cleaned the fish, he put them, with everything he'd just mentioned (he also listed: four liters of dry wine, one liter of sweet white wine, and one liter of the purest oil) into a big, cast-iron casserole dish and sealed its lid with a handful of wet ashes. All of it, he said, he left to cook

over a low fire for the whole afternoon. But while the dish was cooking—
and this explained why he'd served the meal a little late, for which he
apologized—he'd had a new inspiration. He went back to the guts he'd
discarded and pulled out all the fattest livers and all the bits of offal from
the smallest fish. He noticed a very distinct, bitter odor; he ran the full
stream of water from the faucet over these livers and bits of offal for what
might have been more than an hour. Finally, having squeezed out the
water, he began to chop. After reducing everything to a paste, he gradually
added four tablespoons of red vinegar. Then he waited for a couple more
hours. When he knew it was time, he unsealed the lid of his casserole and
ladled out all the liquid. With great care he began separating the flesh of
the fish from the bones (which he called spines) and placed the differently
colored pieces into a deep dish, arranging them in a whimsical fashion
dictated by the colors of the fish themselves. Leaving the deep dish in the
oven for a minute, he returned to the preparation of the sauce. He mixed
the juice he'd removed from the casserole into the paste of livers, offal, and
vinegar. He enhanced its smoothness by mashing up, with the mortar and
pestle, all the little bits and pieces of fish flesh that were too tiny to incor-
porate into the overall structure. Finally, he poured the sauce over what
he'd placed in the deep dish. Since the pieces of fish had been judiciously
arranged, they were entirely covered in this thick sauce, which he'd made
sure he kept simmering in the oven until he poured it out. And voilà!

"Are you married?" the captain asked Monsieur Hour once Quéréjéta had left. No, Hour wasn't married, and his parents were still living at
Bois-Colombes. "They have a private income," he said. His father kept a

garden for pleasure. Trocelier was married. "But," he said, "my wife is in Afghanistan." "A strange place for a woman," said Larreguy. "She's doing archaeological research," said Trocelier, "with the Mitrot-Devesset expedition. It's sad we have diplomas that require us to be this far apart." Hers was in Asian languages. Naturally, Larreguy and Jaurena weren't married. "But," said the captain, "Larreguy lived for three months at Saint-Jean-du-Var, in a suburb with vegetable gardens, with no glass balls." "With no glass balls, monsieur," said Larreguy, "but not far from some olive groves I've told you were as beautiful as the gardens of Armida." "Exactly," said the captain, "you said so, and I believe it, but you did have a Casino chain store fifty meters away." "It didn't interfere with the gardens of Armida." "I'll go even further," said the captain. "It was indispensable to the gardens of Armida. That's what I meant to say." "I assume," said Larreguy, "you'll want to give us the opportunity to measure the events we witness against that scale." "What scale?" asked Trocelier. Larreguy then told them about the conversation he'd had with the captain a few days earlier, when they were coming back from the spot where the sounding line had towed the dinghy away. "Just like it helps to have a human figure in a photo of the Eiffel Tower, to give a sense of scale," he said, "the captain made it possible for me to realize the magnitude of what we'd witnessed, with the help of a grocery store outlet and the glass balls people put in gardens."

"As for myself," said the captain, "I am married. I even have two daughters, and they themselves are married. Right now my wife is probably at the home of her favorite son-in-law, in Périgueux, stroking her grandchildren's pink bottoms. As I told Monsieur Larreguy, I want to give the loveliest gifts I can to those grandchildren. Most of their generation, if they make out well in life, will be able to go on living only in imagination. They need to know reality is more fantastic than imagination...to know they live in a world more vibrant than a playing card, and more flavorful than that fish sauce of Quéréjéta's. I want to free them from the little kitchen garden, from the glass ball, from the grocery store outlet, from the railway station wicket, from everything that makes up their garden of Armida.

"There's nothing unknown in this world anymore. Every new generation is forced to fabricate the exceptional and the unfamiliar for itself, through wars and big, militaristic institutions. We've already entered the era of monstrosities these troubles lead to. Like the Aztecs, we've been obliged to create the political divinities we feed with raw infants in order to stir ourselves up a little. Because we lack imagination (it's fallen away from us, like vestigial limbs fall away from other species), we're incapable of giving these monsters the powers and colors of the plumed serpent, or the fiery bronze of Moloch. We take an ordinary man and, through our stupidity, we grant him so much sway over us that he devours us, but with ugliness. To tell you the truth, it's not a scientific voyage I set out on."

He let a lengthy silence go by, and then added: "I set out to travel around the very places that must once have been a prodigious paradise. I want us to be the witnesses who can confirm we still have the right to a delirium that can enrich the longest lives and make us love even the onset of death.

"I want us to be the first to become drunk on this sacred absinthe that used to fill the gardens of the earth."

Following this, Monsieur Larreguy remarked on the strange transformation in Quéréjéta's face. "His voice," he said, "is the same, but I doubt, if he went back to his village of Esparza, a single young woman would recognize him.

"However," he continued, "if I met him as he is now, on the street of a town, even a town in Chile, he'd remind me of where I come from, by the look of his face alone. Out toward Londaïsbehere there's a stone they call 'the carved stone.' It used to mark the boundary of the common pastureland. It has four sides and each one bears a sculpted face that's round and gold, exactly like his face is now." Jaurena agreed, but pointed out that the same kind of boundary stones were found near Olçomendy, and, in the village of Landarretche, all the old houses had keystones, above their doors, carved with the same, rounded visage. He added that Landarretche means "the poor man's house." But the captain politely asked that they talk no further, and as soon as the meal was done, he went to bed.

The captain, who, as usual, had spent the night reading, had fallen asleep toward morning, when he was awakened by cries and the hurried trampling of crew members on deck. The sun was up, but the light was murky. His watch read 7:00. There was a knock at his door, and before he could ask if the weather was foul, Monsieur Larreguy shouted for him to hurry to come and see an extraordinary spectacle.

He ran up on deck wearing his red dressing gown. "I had to show you this cloud rising from the southwest," said Larreguy. "It's moving in a singular fashion." "You shouldn't think I can give you an explanation for everything," said the captain. But when he looked closely at the phenomenon, he could tell there was something remarkable about it.

Considerably darker than an ordinary storm cloud, it blocked out the sky completely, and it was so opaque, it had almost plunged the space below it into night. From around the cloud's edges, a sheaf of sunbeams escaped to vanish into the far northwestern reaches. The light was hidden over hundreds of square kilometers of ocean that had become as dark as pitch. But the oddest thing was the unusual pulsation that made the cloud throb as it traveled through the sky. Its motion was no longer regular and impersonal, like it would be if it were imparted by the winds, but seemed endowed with intelligence, rocking now right, now left, as though to lean against the mass of the air and finally launch itself at prodigious speed in the general direction of the north.

Sometimes the sunlit edges turned white and appeared to hurl smoke or spray, of dazzling whiteness, under the cloud's dark belly. But these faded out after a moment, when they penetrated further into the shadow they cast. They appeared so quickly, and you immediately heard the sound they made. It was a sort of fluid rumbling. Finally, in this rumbling, the men made out a sound similar to oil frying in a pan.

However, there wasn't the least bit of wind, and the water was completely flat over considerable stretches. Even under the advancing cloud, the water was so still, you could detect, far off to the south, the white belly of the dead sperm whale, which continued to drift without the slightest trace of waves breaking against it, as though it had drifted away in oil. The rollers, which hadn't stopped battering the rocky coastline even during the calmest weather, had subsided, and for the first time the ear was no longer disturbed by the explosions of waves crashing in the mouths of the caverns.

Nevertheless, the cloud kept moving steadily and remarkably fast. It was about to reach the summit of the volcano, when everyone realized it was an immense cloud of birds. Streaming in bands, like enormous, black scarves, they wound themselves two or three times around the sides of the island. Then, with a noise of wings and cries, they plunged the ship into utter darkness, passing within a hundred meters of the masts to go and settle a mile or two away, all at once, on the surface of the sea, which they covered in an instant.

Remnants of this strange squadron were still racing overhead, but now the sun and the azure sky were filling the gaps in the cloud of birds, and shafts of lovely daylight began to strike the huge expanse of wings and feathers that had landed on the sea.

Half an hour later, all the birds had landed on the water and fallen silent. The new light of a fine, southern spring day burst into the cloudless sky.

They were almost exclusively albatrosses and snow petrels. The captain explicitly forbade the firing of rifles and he advised all the crew and officers, several times, to take care to remain within earshot. He ordered them to continue to fish at their leisure, as they'd begun to do the day before, but advised them to do so only in the vicinity of the ship.

He questioned Monsieur Trocelier closely about the pathways that would permit them to gain access to the first ledges overlooking the cliffs. He appointed a ship's guard led by Baléchat, along with Gorri and Marchais. For his personal shore party, he retained all his officers, plus three sailors, including master carpenter Braibant. Archigard and Paumolle were the others. For these seven selected men, as well as himself, he asked Larreguy to pack provisions of food and drink for two days. He advised this special team, over which he stated he was taking command, to furnish themselves with arms and ammunition: service revolvers for the officers, and a submachine gun for Archigard, with its ammunition to be carried by the other two sailors. He made it clear that the dinghy should be constantly at the ready to come and carry away this shore team of which he was a part. He pointedly asked Trocelier to tell him, in his opinion, how long it would take to reach the basalt shelf above the cliff, and having received the answer, he said they could eat their midday meal without hurrying. All of these precautionary measures proved unnecessary. During the course of the day, from the rock shelf they could observe the huge flock of birds staying settled on the sea, like snow on a moor. The flock didn't dive, and it let itself be rocked, without a sound, by the undulations of the backwash. The sailors didn't even see the birds ruffle themselves to dip and feed. No doubt, the extreme fatigue of the journey they'd made to get here had forced them to drop down suddenly, powerless, like snowflakes. Nevertheless, in spite of the backwash and the motion of the waves, they stayed always in the same place. They must have been paddling in unison with their webbed feet, in order not to be carried away from the spot where they'd come down.

This was one of the calmest days the ship had spent in Falmouth Bay. Over considerable distances in all directions the water was like a mirror, and soon, even underneath the huge patch of birds, the backwash stopped rocking.

All day long the sailors kept lowering lines again and easily caught large numbers of green, sardine-sized fish with shaggy heads as big as a man's fist. These fish were horribly ugly. For several hours they couldn't be gotten rid of—they were as pesky as flies—and as soon as they were caught, they were so unpleasant to look at, the men threw them right back into the sea as far away possible. No matter if the men moved to a new spot, the water all around was muddied with these fish, down to a great depth. Amazingly, even the albatrosses and petrels didn't try to eat them. It was Archigard who finally decided that, if you cut their heads off, they looked decent enough. So the men caught a barrelful and immediately soaked them in brine. They buried the heads in a pit on the beach. They were happy as well to catch a sort of red mullet, and finally—with a bottom line Paumolle had set close to the sheer walls of the cliff—a medium-sized conger eel, which thrashed the water with violence.

It was the movements of this fish that made them notice the exceptional calmness of the day. As soon as they'd hauled the creature aboard and stunned it, they saw that all the foam it had whipped up during its fight had already merged into the incredibly flat, oily surface of the ocean, which was making unbroken contact with the rocks precisely at the high-water mark, like a carpet.

Strangest of all was the silence of the birds. Throughout the day the captain was constantly visiting one fisherman after another and keeping an eye on the bay; he even started to climb onto the rocks to the north. First, he shaded his eyes with his hand to be able to look into the sun, and then, with his spyglass, he closely observed the whole aquatic bird encampment.

You'd have said they were sleeping; but, from time to time, they dipped their heads rapidly in the water, then lifted them back up. They made no other motions. They were spread out, in a single mass, over a very broad expanse. The men saw the captain putting his spyglass back into its case. He jumped down from his rock onto the sand and began striding along the beach to get back to the dinghy and return to the ship.

He'd assigned Paumolle to the crow's nest. Now the men could see him up there, smoking his pipe, as calmly as if he were sitting in a tree firmly planted in the ground. The sea was so still, and the mast so motionless, that the smoke from his pipe stayed suspended around his face. The captain ventured into the upper shrouds, where they saw him performing a sort of semaphore in order to pull out his spyglass and look again in the direction of the birds.

In the evening, he relieved everyone from duty, and they all went to bed. A small night watch was left on deck, composed of seamen Hervéou and Brodier, along with Archigard, who asked to join them, claiming he couldn't sleep.

As usual the night blanketed itself with stars, and the atmosphere became close right away. To get as much fresh air as possible, the three men went to sit at the highest point of the prow. In addition to the two navigation lights and a stationary lantern affixed to the mainmast at eye level, they had a smaller lantern, which cast a reddish light at their feet.

It was past midnight when the ship moved a little. The bow had slowly lifted, as if it had ridden over a minor obstacle. Archigard leaned over the rail and swung his lantern out at arm's length. He could see a silent, rounded ridge of blackish water. Cresting slowly, it parted around the prow before washing two or three times onto the sand beach with a soft, hissing sound. The vessel swayed twice, slowly and noiselessly. Then came back to rest.

Ahead of the bow, in spite of the darkness, the birds had just taken flight. They hadn't gained enough momentum to raise themselves high into the air; they'd simply lifted themselves a few meters above the water, where they circled, as one, making no sound other than the muffled beating of thousands of wings. Then, circling back over the bay, they came and dropped down as one, in the spot they'd left.

Up until that moment, everything had been so strangely calm, the muffled sound of the birds' flight was enough to make the captain, Monsieur Larreguy, and Monsieur Jaurena appear suddenly in the hatchway. The watch informed them of what had just taken place. The ship was steady once again. However, now they could hear the water bubbling several hundred meters ahead, underneath the birds. It was impossible to see what was going on out there. Whatever it was, it seemed to be something peaceful, and it was reasonable to assume that, after the birds had recovered from their exhaustion, they'd begun to feed on the school of big-headed green fish.

Around five in the morning, Gorri and Baléchat relieved the watch. Archigard stayed up, smoking his little black pipe. From time to time, he raised his lantern toward the open water and tried to peer into the darkness, which, little by little, was now becoming grey. Gorri and Baléchat were making themselves some coffee, when Archigard came and informed them it was ice. "What?" they asked. The thing the birds were on: it was a sort of long chunk of ice that rose barely a meter above the water, and all the birds were resting on it.

In the early morning light, it was hard to see the thing clearly, but, indeed, the birds did seem to be resting on a pearly grey mass that, in certain places, had the golden-brown highlights of ice from southern latitudes. However, it was ice that must have been lapped for a long time by warm water, because it no longer had any sharp edges. Instead, it was so rounded, it looked like a vast tortoise shell under the birds.

As the sun grew higher and the birds took off in long, fluttering banners, you could see this chunk of ice must have been about two or three hundred meters long, by a good fifty wide. But even though there wasn't the least movement in the water, which remained diabolically calm, at times you could see, as though they were being stirred by movements from deep below, some protruding bits of ice. These were much farther away than the spot where the birds had gathered; and gradually, as if it were being lifted from below, the ice appeared much longer than it had seemed when it first came into view.

It took a long time for the three sailors to realize that the white mass over which the birds were wheeling and landing was moving on it own. Not only did it sometimes raise itself out of the sea, three or four meters taller than it had seemed to be, and then collapse and submerge entirely, leaving a wake of short-lived waves and eddies; it also stretched itself out, making humps and serrated undulations emerge far ahead and race across the sea like the sinuous progress of a snake.

The men had to look over and over again at the oily, impenetrable, utterly placid water around the hull of the ship, and at the glittering mirror of the unruffled sea, before they realized, abruptly, that this ice seemed to be alive.

This was when a strange, white strap, as thick as a brine barrel and more than a hundred meters long, lifted into the air, whistling like an enormous whip. Cleaving a dense flock of petrels in two, it fell back into the water with a dull thud, surrounded by gushes of spume and steam. In a single bound, the three sailors of the watch dove down the hatch. For a good while, the deck remained deserted. No one had extinguished the mainmast lantern. When he came up from below, the captain's first act was to extinguish it. Then he went forward and climbed onto the prow.

He was wearing his red dressing gown and some slippers. Behind him, Larreguy was buttoning his peacoat. "Well, well," said the captain, "here it is, I believe, our fine bit of nasty business."

"Is it a corpse?" asked Larreguy. "I don't believe so," said the captain. "And so much the better. If it were a corpse, it wouldn't take long for it to start stinking. And it's too big for us to be able to get away from the stink so easily. Besides, there's no reason why this animal should be dead. It's the first time, I believe, anyone has ever seen one on the surface. Here, take a look."

At this point, the white animal once again sent one of its enormous, white tentacles hissing through the air. "It's monstrous," said Larreguy. "What is it you're looking for?" asked the captain. "Do you remember how I refused to load the harpoon gun they offered to us when we were leaving?" he continued. "I commend myself for it. No doubt, we would have wanted to fire it now, into this white mass covered in birds. That's just what you're looking around for, isn't it?" "Yes," said Larreguy, "a weapon!" "Well, well," said the captain, "don't we already have one? We have no need of powder, explosion, cannon, and shell. Let's just watch and enjoy the thing. Remember your angels. Do you still want to fire cannons at angels?"

As the sun continued to rise, the animal began moving slowly through the water. Little by little it spread six thick tentacles around its head and stretched them forward. All along them, the birds immediately dropped down and began pecking away, like they'd already done, with shrieks and in battle array, on top of the big, scarab-shaped body of the animal, which was so vast it resembled an island.

"So, in this way," said Monsieur Larreguy, "it lets itself be eaten alive by the birds." "I don't think so," said the captain. "It's a simple cleaning operation. This fine fellow has come up to the surface to have himself cleaned. What I haven't managed to figure out, yet, is who set the time. This is what it would be interesting to know. Did this creature—by some mysterious warning, of which we were perfectly unconscious—tell the birds, for thousands of kilometers around, to come en masse to the place where he was going to surface? Or did he sense from below, in the shadowy depths, the birds calling, and the darkness hanging under their cloud?

"What's important, and what fascinates me now, is to understand how this huge dweller of the ocean floor could have informed the birds. Just look at them: it looks like they're playing a game!"

It was indeed a monstrous and impressive game being played between the huge white squid and the whole host of birds, which were as white as he was. Given his enormous mass, he needed heavy movements to shift his long arms and wave his palpi, the flaps he used to travel smoothly through the water. The birds gathered on him were pecking over his entire body. From time to time they'd take off in a cloud, shifting their position and leaving the animal's skin, in the places where they'd sat, as clean and white as snow. Sometimes one of the long, tentacular arms would rise up toward one of these flights of birds, and while the flock was wheeling about, the huge, white strap seemed to be seeking it out in order to caress it, to charm it. As soon as the tentacle crashed back down onto the calm surface, oblivious to the foam and spume it would send up, the birds came down with it and started right away to peck at it with fervor. Looking at this game through the spyglass, you could tell the birds were feeding on a layer of kelp, shellfish, and tiny, teeming organisms that completely covered the squid.

In the sunlight, in the places the birds had cleaned, the skin of the completely white animal began to show the sort of iridescence that flashes from millraces and the silvered backs of mirrors.

"And there's the smell," said Monsieur Larreguy. "I've been aware of it for a while," said the captain, "but I can't say what it's like. On the day when I examined the contents of the sperm whale's gut, I was already struck by the novelty of the smell. You can't say it's unpleasant, and at first, it's really quite agreeable. But you can't say what it's like." "Spring," said Larreguy. "Spring," said the captain, "yes. But spring what? Not violets, not the narcissus scent of our giant ray. Not the sweet-smelling-corpse scent of spring, this time. A flower? A tree? A grass? What? What does it make you think of?"

"Nothing," said Larreguy, "it's an unfamiliar smell. Unless, perhaps, it gives a general sense of spring." "Yet there's nothing springlike," said the captain, "about this great hulking oaf that's as white as snow, with a hundred thousand petrels pecking at its hide. Look at it, and tell me if there's anything springlike about it."

And the white monster—almost the whole of its back having been cleaned now from top to bottom—began to roll over on its side, bringing its sticky, glistening, cartilaginous plates above the surface. With a sort of spasmodic satisfaction, the creature seemed to be stretching itself out, and more and more often it was swinging the full length of its tentacles. But now, instead of lifting them and flinging them down like a whiplash onto the water, it let them float idly up in the sunshine, raising them almost straight up into the air, rotating them so that they showed their huge rows of pink suckers. Sometimes the creature's arms lazily and knowingly went after the flocks of birds that were wheeling around it. At one point, what looked like long fingers of gold thrust out in bunches from the tips of the tentacles. These fingers would suddenly wrap around an albatross and hold it prisoner. The bird would struggle at first, but then its neck and wings would go limp. The gold fingers then unclenched and let the dead bird drop into the sea. With each of the animal's movements (by now it was almost turned over on its back), the heavy smell would drench the ship.

"Despite everything," said Monsieur Larreguy, "what this smell most clearly reminds me of is spring." "I have to agree," said the captain. "That's my impression too. But I can't figure out why. Spring has a meaning! Spring what? Spring humus? Humus warmed by the first sunshine in May? Rains? Rains that have swept through miles and miles of flowering trees of every kind and march horizontally across the land, driven by the wind? Is that the smell, Monsieur Larreguy?" "No," said Larreguy, "spring..." "I know damn well," said the captain, "but I ask you again, spring what? It's a spring smell for me too, this stifling smell. But I'm not satisfied with that. I can't manage to figure out the connection this smell can have with spring on land."

"It has no relation," said Larreguy, "but it's a spring fragrance all the same. It's much more expressive than any of the spring fragrances I've ever known on land. What I can tell you is that it affects me in a way that's quite characteristic of springtime." "Indeed," said the captain, "it's been many months now since we left behind the charming companions who must fill your leisure hours, as a young, unmarried man, with magic." "That's exactly what I meant," said Larreguy, "however, I assure you, it hasn't caused me any hardship so far." "And it took wallowing in this foul cesspool to make you remember them?" "I'm sorry," said Larreguy, "but that is, in fact, the exact physical sensation I'm having. Insofar as we need to try to explain the springlike quality of the scent we're inhaling..." "To hell with 'if we need to!'" said the captain. "It's the most important thing of all. You don't need to excuse yourself. It's exactly the sensation I've been feeling myself, despite my fifty years. So there's no need to feel ashamed. This infernal force from the sea seems to be explaining some dark matters to us, with eloquence. Despite all our intelligence, we're still only grasping them as hints, and even so, they're already damned frightening."

Now the squid was completely rolled over on its back. It was raising its extraordinarily viscous, supple underbelly—on which birds were getting stuck and thrashing about now and then—above the surface. Flocks of still vigorous petrels and albatrosses were attempting, by violently flapping their wings, to break away from this glistening glue that coated the whole belly of the squid. The smell had become more and more distinct. At last the captain, looking through his spyglass, noticed, near the center of the monster's belly, a whorl of sunken flesh from which a sticky, whitish liquid was issuing in spurts. The part of the monster visible above the surface was traversed by strange quiverings that generated concentric rings of waves, like those set off when a stone hits the water. As this glue was pouring out, flooding the squid's belly and saturating the birds, the smell had become frighteningly distinct.

It smelled of pancake dough, chestnut blossom, wet flour, stale egg, sprouted wheat. A kind of intoxication seemed to have taken hold of the birds. As heavier and heavier streams of this glue-like substance poured out, the birds dashed themselves against the squid's belly, striking it with their wings and their beaks. They rose in dense eddies, high into the sky, full of cries and agitation that made them fight one another and fall, like dead weights, onto the squid's white hide, which was now as slimy as a marsh.

Each time, large numbers of birds remained stranded, thrashing their wings in this secretion, which flowed more and more abundantly from the fleshy, open slot in the mollusk's belly. The birds held prisoner in this way made ghastly efforts, all together, to get free from the muddy, smelly secretion. You could see the remarkable convulsions with which they all tried to widen their wings and stretch out their necks, but the birds were so numerous and so entangled with each other, and the secretion was gushing over them in such abundant streams, it wasn't long before they drowned in it.

A thick layer of dead, stranded birds remained glued to the belly of the squid. From moment to moment, stronger and stronger streams were issuing from the leathery belly, as swirls of increasingly inebriated birds crashed down and tried to get away with outstretched wings, only to end up hopelessly mired.

The frighteningly distinct odor must now have covered a considerable stretch of ocean. The birds were no longer settled on the water like a dusting of white. Instead, as though shaped by the wind of the extraordinary, appalling tempest, they were gathering into columns and soaring up in a dense jet, climbing all together, in desperation, to an elevation that seemed even higher than the volcano of Tristan.

When one of these columns passed in front of the sun, it cast a shadow as upright as a tree trunk.

It was up there, high in the azure, that the nethermost tip of these upwellings of birds finally curled over like the crest of a wave, and the whole, dense column collapsed, in a cacophony of cries, onto the motionless belly of the squid, from which the bubblings of sweet-smelling muck continued to surge and pour. Right away, the masses of birds already stranded were joined by new masses of quivering wings and feathers, and then they too finally died in the quagmire, their wings strangely extended in their last paroxysms of life.

This continued all morning. Neither the sailors, nor the captain, nor the officers dreamt of making the slightest move in front of the spectacle. At most, from time to time, and without speaking a word, the captain passed his spyglass to Monsieur Larreguy.

Toward the middle of the day, the eruptions of birds were getting more and more dense. However, a horrific layer of wings and feathers, covering the belly of the squid, began to collapse slowly, from both sides, into the sea.

The birds were cemented into a huge bundle that stayed intact in the lapping of the sea, which was beginning to be stirred by a westerly breeze. The rolling of the water sometimes lifted the enormous mass of the floating mollusk, and little by little, it seemed to take advantage of the rolling to spread itself out more and more widely on the surface. In this way it enlarged the huge marsh, smelling of pollen, in the muck where the birds were dying. Extremely slowly, the monstrous animal finally raised, one after the other, the seven long arms covered in tentacles that were spread out over hundreds of meters. It started to raise them, one by one, like the fingers of a gigantic hand, and held them there that way, upright, in the air.

The columns of birds didn't cease soaring up to amazing heights. Sometimes, like the tendrils of a vine around a stake, one or two of the squid's long arms wrapped around the upsurging birds. But their dashes toward the sky were so vigorous, and the strength of their wings carried them so quickly to the upper reaches, that the squid's tentacles never took hold of anything solid and passed right through the flock as if it were made of smoke.

Ever since this stuff that smelled like wet flour had begun to spurt out of the squid's belly, the birds had started to cry so stridently that the non-stop noise had plugged all the sailors' ears, exactly as if it were silence. Apart from the slight undulation of the water, stirred by the light breeze out of the west, everything was profoundly calm. The birds' upwelling itself, though propelled by an incredibly rapid impulse, was so distinctive and had lasted for so long, the column itself had become a calm presence dissolved in the immensities of the sky and the sea.

As for the movements of the enormous tentacles, they were so supple, so slow, so weightless and slack, in time it became impossible to distinguish them from the stillness all around them.

Nothing seemed to be in motion, neither the upwellings of the birds, nor the flailings of the huge, white whiplashes; nor did anything seem to have arrived from anywhere, or to have arisen from anywhere; but everything was there, like the immutable presence of the sky and the sea. Nothing appeared to be out of place. On the contrary, everything was exceptionally coherent. Even more intently than they were watching the strangeness of the spectacle, all of the men were gazing, without growing weary, and oblivious of the passage of time, at the open sea, which lay calmly between the four bare horizons.

Toward noon Quéréjéta came up from the storeroom and was about to ring the two bells for the midday meal. But he let go of the rope right away, without having made a sound, and walked to the taffrail on his soft, worn slippers. From here, he too began watching the spectacle, heedless of the hour.

Just as the sun was plummeting to the horizon, the men saw two or three long, bluish sparks shoot up from the squid. They made a soft, slapping sound in the still air. Then, as night fell—all at once, as usual—they saw a sort of pale halo quiver and pulse from the monster, in waves of light curving like a rainbow, and the mollusk raised above itself a great dome of whitish phosphorescence.

Once again it had lowered its long arms into the sea, and while the sludge of dying birds stayed glued to its belly and new columns were endlessly crashing down with shrill cries, it began slowly to tread the water with its monstrous limbs, making strange splashes of golden light shoot up from the surface. Soon the squid ended up kneading together sea-water with large bunches of the birds stuck in this liquid seed, which smelled like flour. Gradually, the animal made an incredible bed of light and fire boil up around itself. Amid spray and radiant scum, the seething bed became covered with the dismembered bodies of dead birds, their wings outspread.

Without interruption, the dark silhouette of the birds, which seemed crucified by their final efforts to free themselves from the quagmire, stood out against the sea, lit up now and rolling gently with the swell. Their protracted agony had hardened them like iron.

At times the slight rocking of the water made their bodies lift halfway above the surface, and then the light emanating from the squid would start to glisten across their wing feathers. Suddenly the whole expanse over which the squid was spread seemed to be bristling with iridescent crystals.

The softly bursting, bluish flashes kept on erupting from the white hide of the mollusk, and then, all at once, the whole, uplifted column of birds would light up. It stood there, upright, quivering and blue, like the trunk of a palm tree going up in flames.

The light emanating from the creature wasn't a mere phospho-rescence; it was like the beam projected from an immense lantern. It reached as far as the ship and even beyond, to the island and all the way to the cabins at the base of the cliffs.

Toward the middle of the night, the squid began slowly to roll over, and when it exposed its belly facing the ship, the sailors could see that the aperture had stopped disgorging the glue that had held the birds prisoner.

A moment later, the creature rolled all the way onto its belly, and you could see in an instant that the glow emanating from the animal was an extraordinary light that had been shaded until now by a thick tangle of feathers and wings; because, as soon as the clean bare back of the animal emerged, a bright and vivid radiance spread out in every direction over the sea and, rising higher than the ship's masts, reached all the way to the top of the cliffs.

Caught unawares, the rest of the birds who were still capable of flying ceased mounting their column and dropped like rain into the illuminated sea.

Abruptly, once the birds stopped crying, the pure silence gave the sailors a start, as though it were a real sound. Now, as high as they could see into the heavens lit up by the squid, the sky was empty. Once in a while, bluish flashes shot out from the creature and soared into the darkness like rainbows, then went on to merge with the grey halo that encompassed the scene.

It was thanks to one of these flashes that the men noticed the creature was gradually spinning around, and it wouldn't be long before it was directly facing the bay where the ship was anchored. Soon, in the middle of the huge, white mass on whose surface the luminous force was continually flickering and occasionally emitting flashes, they saw an enormous, black globe emerge. Everything was lit up, except for this globe that projected above the shape that broke the surface. And this globe was as black as tar. Gradually, as the animal turned to face them more and more directly, they saw what looked like little windows of light appearing in this black globe, and finally they realized it was an eye. And, as the reflected light seemed to reveal, this lidless eye was staring directly ahead.

Instinctively, the men looked around, and they realized with dread that the light from the squid was strong enough to make each of them cast a clear shadow. Moreover, the ship itself cast a shadow with its masts all the way to the walls of the cliff. Gradually, the creature, continuing to swing around, showed its two eyes to the ship. Both of these eyes were getting bigger, so the men knew the creature was heading toward them in the darkness.

Little by little, it dimmed its light. Soon, down there below them, it was no longer anything more than a small, half-extinguished phosphorescence, barely strong enough to reveal the two, huge, motionless eyes. Slowly welling up from the sea, a slender strap, pale and long, which was only the lit-up edge of an enormous tentacle, floated languidly into the air and, tracing against the night stars a figure-eight arabesque that endlessly tied and untied itself, approached the ship through the darkness.

With their eyes raised, they followed this strap until it was over top of the ship. It must have struck the mast, because the vessel suddenly jumped on its keel like a shying horse, and at the same time, the huge tentacle, weighing several tons, was suddenly lit up in its entirety. They could see it in the air, barely a few meters above their heads, fluttering like the lash of a whip. And right then the huge bunch of six tentacles, more blinding than rockets, shot up to dizzying heights. And while the whole crew was reeling in disarray on the deck, everything faded out in a hissing of quenched embers. They could hear the sea sloshing as it filled a large void.

In the pitch darkness, the men were calling out to each other. "Lights!" cried the captain. "The lanterns are all lit," came the voice of Monsieur Larreguy. "It's this damned plunge into darkness that's blinded us." In fact, little by little, they were beginning to make out the deck of the ship under the navigation lights and the mainmast lantern. "Who lit them?" asked the captain. "I did," said the voice of Noël Guinard.

It was hard to tell if the faded creature was still breaking the surface out there. In the darkness they heard only occasional flights of birds; birds that were passing by the island heading north. The men had begun to hear the rollers again, booming against the cliff. A stiff, southerly breeze had suddenly picked up. The ship started to drift slowly over its anchor, and then, having stretched the chain, it came to a stop, still rocking a little. No stars shone. Sounds became louder and louder, as though they were bellowing from the vault of some cavern; then suddenly, fat, round, warm drops of water were splattering everywhere. It was raining.

VIII

Rain

ALL NIGHT LONG the rain falls in heavy sheets, which the men hear raging across the deck. At times there are lulls when the roar of ocean waves, breaking against the cliffs on both sides of the bay, is carried by the wind. Then, in the distance, the next sheet of rain starts to hiss as it approaches. It pours down and tramples everything. The seams between the planks, which during a month at anchor had been drying in the sun, have opened up. Right away drops begin falling everywhere belowdecks, as heavily in the captain's cabin as in the officer's wardroom, the sailors' berths, and Quéréjéta's galley. The drops are ringing off floorboards, sea chests, saucepans, cauldrons, crates; smacking on leather book bindings and on hanging clothes; and slowly but surely the very smell of rain takes over the whole interior of the ship.

Day breaks late, revealing a ceiling of cloud with mists hanging low enough to touch the tip of the mainmast, and the slanting streaks of a relentless rain. A fair, steady breeze starts to tear at the sea foam.

Since dawn the sunlight has barely increased. Now it's steady, obscured only by incoming sheets of rain. Although the cloud ceiling is a uniform grey, these sheets of rain, hanging like the tines of a harrow, wander calmly here and there across the surface of the sea. They're suspended, dark and slanted, and in the places where they touch down, the water spurts up steam and froth, which the wind then carries away. Each time one of these squalls comes into the bay and strikes the ship, the stern rears back, and the whole vessel shudders from keel to topmast like a horse that balks. Torrents of rain drench the ship, sometimes from forward, sometimes from starboard, sometimes from port, and rock it back and forth. Then they move away across the bay, where they trample vast stretches of water and cause the blades and stems of a huge belt of kelp to appear.

The captain has tried to find a dry place to hang his dressing gown. But he's been repeatedly obliged to remove it from every corner of the cabin. He has no other option but to stuff it under his bedding. His blanket is wet, his sheets are wet, his smock is wet, his slippers are filling up with water. He opens his sea chest to take out his rubber boots. His head his wet, his hair is wet. He picks up his cap and has to empty it out; it was upside down in his chest and had already filled up with water. He takes out his boots and his oilskin. He carefully half-opens the lid of his chest to reach for one of his thick, wool sweaters. He grabs it quickly, pressing it against his chest; he'll stuff it into his bed next to his dressing gown. That way, he'll have something dry to get into later. Just as carefully, he removes a flannel shirt, and this too he stuffs under his blanket, which is already wet. He spreads out his greatcoat, puts on his smock, pulls his oilskin over top, gets into his boots, covers his head with his sou'wester, and climbs up on deck.

They need to be wary of the stern rearing straight downward each time a sheet of rain beats down on the ship. The captain has the men take a sounding. There are still seven meters of water below the keel. There's no risk that the stern will touch bottom. Nevertheless, they have to expect some drift, as the ship is moored to a single chain. He orders the rowboat to be lowered, and soundings to be taken in the surrounding waters into which the ship could drift if it drags its anchor.

Monsieur Jaurena sets off with two seamen on this sounding expedition. They aren't yet ten meters from the ship before the rain completely erases them from the world. Through the dense streaks of rain, you can barely make out the glistening but unchanging forms of the rowboat and the three oilskins.

In the bay, though, a low, stiff swell seems to be rocking them hard enough. Or is the rain diluting their color and appearance so much that it's making them disappear at times, as if they've been swallowed up in the trough of a swell? It looks, however, like the waves do lift them higher at times, and you can see their oilcloths glistening above the gunwale of the boat. A moment later, in the place where you'd just seen them glistening, there's no longer anything but a white patch. It could be an unusual reflection from the foam, or maybe it's *the gap in the world* they made before they vanished.

The rolling of the ship at anchor is hard to bear. It's not that the vessel is being lifted by the water, it's that she's being crushed under the brutal downpour. So the ship seems to be rearing back on her hind legs, like a horse. And when she rises again, horselike, she arches and stiffens her back to withstand the waves that beat an explosive drum roll on the bottom of the hull.

Now they can't seem to see Monsieur Jaurena's rowboat. It's unlikely he could be taking soundings in any useful way. In keeping with the captain's orders, he hasn't gone more than two hundred meters to the west. This is the only area they might drift to, if they happen to drag the anchor.

"But what we ought to do, monsieur, is call out and tell him not to get too far out of sight to the west. In this rain, it could be impossible to steer clear of the cross-currents at the mouth of the bay."

The captain shouts through his bullhorn, but with the rain, his voice breaks up as if it's hitting a wall. In any case, no answer comes from the rowboat. But, during a lull in the rain, they suddenly see the boat, almost at the limit of where it's supposed to go: it's a great swell that's making it lift and plunge. They yell out for it to come back a little toward the left. It doesn't appear to have heard. They hope it's paying close attention to the currents. Especially as it's impossible to know whether the squid is still in the spot where it played all day yesterday with the birds. But today the visibility doesn't extend more than a hundred meters or so from where the rowboat is sitting. What's more, the spitting rain, which doesn't let up between every gust, completely obscures the boat. And more squalls keep arriving from the west to shroud it.

In spite of all this, they're obliged to keep hailing the boat from time to time. But then, little by little, they see it coming back, slowly, still heavily rocked by the swell. Finally, it draws alongside. It's been able to take three soundings. In the whole area where they might drag anchor, they'd be certain not to touch bottom. Now the sheets of rain, heavier and heavier, are falling more and more steadily, and at last, toward midday, an uninterrupted, extremely heavy rain sets in, a rain which no longer has any beginning or end. But the deck planks have swollen and the seams have closed up, so it's no longer raining belowdecks.

They've stretched three tarpaulins above the reservoirs in order to collect rainwater, and you can hear, deep down in the ship, the drumbeat of the streams pouring from the big downspouts into the tanks.

The wind seems like it will keep blowing nonstop from the north. Toward the end of the day, it shifts decisively to the northwest. They have no choice but to leave the bay to take advantage of the favorable wind and embark on the long crossing to Tierra del Fuego.

On the morning of January 25th, the anchor was raised. The weather was unchanged, the sky low and dark, packed with heavy rain squalls racing across the sea. But the wind stayed fair, blowing out of the north, shifting sometimes to the north-northeast. Yet, because the cliffs almost completely sheltered the head of the bay, they had to tow the ship with the rowboat in order to begin making headway. Manned by Archigard, Paumolle, and Brodier, with Gorri at the helm, the boat pulled the ship out beyond the belt of gigantic kelp. They hauled the rowboat back up on board in the thick of the biggest squall they'd witnessed since the rains began, but now the sails were starting to fill, and the ship, stiffening against the breeze with two or three sharp jerks, began to pick up speed in admirable fashion. By 10:00 in the morning, it reached the open sea, leaving Tristan behind to starboard. It had gone hardly any distance before the island was completely obscured by the rain.

All day long they sailed on a good, fast tack, propelled by a wind that seemed made to order. The ship had resumed its regular roll. It was lightly churning its wake, now on one side, now on the other, and flying before the wind like a skater. The wake stretched back in a straight line and disappeared under the constant rain. The sky wasn't lifting anywhere. In the south, on the contrary, it remained dark and opaque all day.

Night fell fast, and they traveled through it at the same speed, on the same tack, without shifting sail. In the morning the sky appeared denser all around, and the lulls in the rain squalls were increasingly rare. It rained heavily, almost without interruption, and the atmosphere was stifling. The rain drove down vertically, hammering the deck of the ship. Even though the sea lay flat, its surface was bubbling everywhere, bursting with the effects of this endless downfall. Without the spray that was being whipped up by the rain, and despite the low, dark sky blocking all four horizons from view, the visibility would have been fairly good, because, during each short period of calm, you could tell that the clouds, which spread over a vast extent, weren't hanging low to the water anywhere. But, as soon as the rain started to fall again, it would stir up the spray, which turned into an opaque and almost impenetrable cloud of steam in every direction.

On the 30th, while the weather remained the same overall, the wind shifted abruptly to due east, then south, and *L'Indien* was obliged to tack back and forth along the latitude of Rio Negro. The variable winds, twisting the heavy showers like the fibers of a rope, forced the ship to execute some uncertain maneuvers.

The wind, however, remained remarkably easy to handle. It blew steadily, never varying in strength. It simply changed direction, like a rushing stream that changes course as it flows through a stretch of sand. It moved from east to south with the same intensity, then blew a short time later from the north, without increasing the severity of its gusts.

On February 4th, the wind began to blow from the east, through rain that didn't alter, didn't vary in strength, stayed equally heavy everywhere. The ship once again made good headway to the southwest.

This time the thrust of the wind seemed to be channeled through a deep groove in the sky. Up ahead, there was always the same trembling opacity of spray and rain, behind which you saw the black backdrop of sky. Astern there was nothing but the wake—as solid as if it were being plowed through snow—which ran for some ten meters and then immediately vanished under the rain.

Throughout the nights the drumming of the rain rolled endlessly on the deck. You started to hear it as soon as darkness flattened the shadows and erased the rippling and spray of the water's surface. This drumming had two pitches—one high, one low—which alternated according to the regular rocking of the ship, and to whether the deck was exposed horizontally, or vertically, to the hammering of the heavy drops of water. It corresponded precisely with the regular swaying of the ship's forward motion. In the morning, when the daylight expanded, the noise subsided and became nothing more than a gentle murmur in the background, which joined the sounds of maneuvers and conversations.

Suddenly the wind came out of the west, along with a little, raging swell, and lashed the ship, all around and above, with heavier and heavier rain. A short, hard swell began pounding in from all sides. That same day the wind, still violent, struck the sails from three different quarters. But, in the evening, it subsided all at once into a perfect calm. The sails, heavy with rain, immediately began to luff. The swell kept knocking against the sides of the ship; then the water turned smooth; and now the men found themselves in an exceptional calm in the midst of a downpour. It was February 10th.

Paumolle is the one who, every morning at 6:00, brings the coffee to the captain and his lieutenants. Paumolle's berth is above Brodier's. Inside the little Breton-style bed where Paumolle sleeps, he's set up, from one wall to the other, a whole cat's cradle of strings. On it he hangs his underwear, which is always clean, because he's particularly partial to cleanliness. He's the one who has the largest set of striped undershirts. Four of them with sleeves, and five without sleeves. The sleeveless ones are low-cut, with narrow shoulder straps, exposing his huge, bare arms and his upper back and shoulders, which are almost black, they've been so roasted by the sun.

Nevertheless, his tan isn't dark enough to mask his conspicuous tattoos, which embellish his skin from wrist to shoulder. On his right arm there's a snake that begins by winding three times around his wrist, and then, enlacing his arm, sinks its fangs into the hollow of his elbow. On the same side, on the broad part of his bicep, there's a heart—pierced by an arrow—that weeps blue blood. Four or five tears of this blue blood drop down into the throat of the snake. In the center of the heart, the name Césarie is inscribed. The heart itself is surrounded by a cluster of leaves, like the leaves of a fan palm, all of them laced with fine veins. To these, the tattooer applied all the delicacy of his art; they bring out the volume of the heart that was pierced by Césarie. Four or five birds soar above this forest. They're finely worked in inks of diverse hues, notably a red that must have been very lovely once, but has turned brick-red on the sunburned skin. All of the birds' feathers have been rendered with great delicacy. You sense the artist was intrigued by the satin-smooth grain and the contours of the skin he'd been asked to cover with his designs. So he also drew, and pricked with inks of every color, three beautiful birds of paradise. To further enhance his vision, he had their long plumes end in foliage that hangs down like the branches of a weeping willow. On Paumolle's shoulders he etched a tortoise shell, and imitation scales cover them like armor. On the left the artist sustained his avian vision, and from wrist to shoulder Paumolle's arm is covered with imaginary birds, which are part birds and part flying trees.

He's very proud of this imagery. Which is why he's more willing to wear his sleeveless undershirts, even when it's cold. What's more, to cap off the poetry and give it its human dimension, Paumolle's neck itself is decorated all the way around with a line of pea-sized dots accompanied by the inscription: "*Tear along dotted line.*"

Bad weather has never prevented Paumolle from doing his laundry.

No storm has ever bothered him, as long as his underwear is clean. As soon as he has a free moment, he tosses out the firkin, hoists up the water, and starts scrubbing. As soon as his underwear is wrung out and clean, he hangs it from the strings he's stretched across his little Breton bed. When he leaves the night watch, before he goes to relax in the forecastle, Paumolle comes and changes his underwear.

On the three wooden panels that enclose his bunk, Paumolle has tacked pictures—cut out of illustrated magazines—which display exclusively women and hunting scenes.

Women of all types found in fashion magazines, sumptuously dressed in furs or evening gowns, covered in jewels, their hair artistically styled, or else in swimsuits, sometimes photographed in color, displaying their firm, tanned flesh above skimpy, flowered costumes clinging to their high hips and ample rumps. There are also cut-out pictures of nude women, no doubt selected from certain exhibitions of paintings. Besides, the figures have all been chosen for their innocence; lounging on sofas, concealing their treasures with an unconcerned hand. On all of these pictures, Paumolle has written the name of Césarie. But you can't conclude anything from this, because he's also written this name, with just as much care, on all the hunting scenes, which alternate with the portraits of women. He has a fine collection of the former; from the loosing of the hounds, to the capture of the quarry. And if he's written the name of Césarie on all of them, in between the horses' hooves and the dogs' and deer's paws, he's also written the name of Césarie on a large portrait of the Duchess of Uzès in full hunting regalia.

Every night Paumolle places his foot on the edge of Brodier's bed, hoists himself with a single pull, and stretches out in his bunk. He lifts his arms, which abound with snakes and birds, puts his hands behind his head, and gazes for a long time at all the Césaries that encircle him.

Brodier, who has taken a good long look at this whole setup, tells him that these horses, these dogs, these deer, and these women are a weird hodgepodge. Not really, Paumolle replies, offhandedly. But every morning when he gets up, Paumolle takes the opportunity, while he climbs down from his bunk, to plant his bare foot on Brodier's face. Brodier wakes up every time, screams every curse he knows, threatens to smash faces in, while Paumolle simply tells him it's just another hodgepodge.

Then, while the men who aren't on watch continue to sleep, Paumolle, still barefoot, leaves, climbs the ladder, and goes to the galley.

There, it's another kind of sideshow. Quéréjéta is making the coffee. And this is a serious business. He makes it after his own fashion, without a coffee pot, in a big cauldron. Using a large wooden spatula, he takes his time stirring the grounds. The key to the whole performance is to bring the mixture to the precise point where it begins to ooze a brown foam, but never to allow the boiling liquid to make this foam burst open. Usually, Paumolle observes the whole procedure without saying a word. When the brew is ready, he knows the exact moment when he has to take hold of the handle of the cauldron to lift it with Quéréjéta and carry it to the table. Then Quéréjéta pours cold water all over the foam, after which it's essential that he bide his time, lost in admiration of the whole upper layer of the beverage, which frees itself gradually of foam and turns smooth and shiny, like a beautiful black lacquer, while the delectable aroma of the morning coffee rises up in steam.

Once the coffee is ready, Quéréjéta lines up four big bowls: one white, one blue, one green, one red. The white is for the captain, the blue for Monsieur Larreguy, the green for Monsieur Jaurena. Quéréjéta and Paumolle share the red one in equal parts. When they've finished, Paumolle picks up the other three bowls.

He has a special method. Because his hands are very broad, he carries two bowls in his right hand, one on his palm and the other gripped by the rim with his thumb and index finger. These two are for the lieutenants. In his left hand he takes only the captain's bowl. It would have to be really bad weather for Paumolle, fitted out like this, to spill even a single drop of coffee, even though he has to climb up one ladder and down another. But it's not clear whether it's for the aroma of the coffee in particular that he's assumed this morning duty, or for the pleasure of being able to play like this, on his own, with the ship. He's already worked out all the ways the ship rolls, depending on the weather. When he arrives at the ladder with the three bowls of coffee, it takes him barely a second to calculate how he has to place his foot on the first rung. In this instant he has to be completely at one with the ship, completely alone on the open seas, and orchestrate a whole series of postures and bracings exactly in harmony with how he needs to balance himself against the swell or the wind. This lasts hardly a moment. Right away his bare foot claps on the first step, and entirely in harmony with the rocking of the world surrounding him, Paumolle mounts the eight rungs of the ladder in a single bound.

It's precisely for the sake of this game that he carries the three coffees to the officers every morning. It really should be Quéréjéta's job instead, or even Brodier's. But at the exact moment when he needs to reflect for a second, to harmonize with the rolling of the rung where he's going to place his foot, it gives him great delight to feel that, in so doing, he can put himself in harmony, from top to toe, with the wind and the waves.

At the head of the ladder, he follows the narrow corridor for three meters, and now here he is at the top of the eight rungs he needs to climb down to get to the little landing where the doors of the three cabins are located. Here he has to use the same magic and perform the same dance in order to get himself to the bottom without spilling a drop of coffee, and then he has to scratch with his toes on the captain's door. Every morning the captain immediately tells him to come in. Paumolle opens the door with his bare foot. His toes are so agile, he can pick up a coin with them just as easily as he can with his fingers. Besides, it's a trick that always wins him a lot of goodwill among the crews he joins. But people get tired of it. This is why he's learned to perform a lot of other amazing bits of mischief with his feet. Once, for a few months, he even tried to roll a cigarette with them. He didn't succeed. But it was no sacrifice, because he made his attempts over a newspaper spread on the floor, and, after each session he always gathered up the tobacco. As for the torn-up cigarette paper, it was no great loss.

When he's told to enter—and every morning, this happens right after he's scratched at the bottom of the door with his toes—he steps back, places his bare foot on the door handle, calmly opens it wide, and enters with a long stride that looks like a dance step. Usually, the captain is sitting on his bed. Smoking his pipe. Sometimes he's reading a book of studies on fish. Or else he might be peacefully smoking, with his hands laid flat in front of him, while he looks without seeing at the big, circular, bluish-green porthole facing him.

This morning, as it sometimes happens, the captain asks Paumolle what the weather's doing. And Paumolle tells him it's raining. The stillness of the ship says clearly enough, on its own, that they're still in a protracted calm.

Even though Paumolle now has his left hand free, he uses his foot again to knock at and open Monsieur Larreguy's door. But sometimes there's no response right away, and he's obliged to rap hard two or three times with his toenails. Besides, Larreguy is always still half asleep, bundled right up to his chin in his blanket, and he barely gives a grunt when Paumolle sets the blue bowl down on the chest that serves as a bedside table.

Sometimes Monsieur Larreguy is on watch at this hour, but more often, like this morning, it's Monsieur Jaurena. So Paumolle carries the green bowl up on deck, where, if nothing extraordinary is going on, he'll usually find Monsieur Jaurena near the helmsman.

This morning the rain is dense and continuous, never weakening, very heavy and very thick. Everything is steaming so much, you can't see overhead any higher than the main yard. From the foot of the mainmast, you can barely make out the dark tip of the prow and the glowing patch of the quarterdeck.

Paumolle has put on a sleeveless undershirt, and right away he gets completely drenched in a warm rain that brings out the satin smoothness of his skin and highlights his tattoos. Jaurena is cloaked in a big, black oilskin, from which the ends of his rubber boots barely stick out. The arrival of the piping hot coffee gives him obvious pleasure. Without blowing on it under the brim of his sou'wester, he gulps it down. Whichever officer is on watch, Paumolle always waits for him to give back the bowl. It wouldn't be good to burden him with anything unnecessary. While he's drinking, Jaurena looks at the finely drawn birds tattooed on Paumolle's left arm, and at the three on his right bicep. He asks him what these birds are, and Paumolle answers that they're games. When Jaurena asks him what kinds of games, "Well," says Paumolle, "bird games, for distraction." "Indeed," says Jaurena, "we do need a bit of distraction." "Do you think, monsieur, we're finally going to get moving today?" "It doesn't look like it," says Jaurena. "We're completely becalmed." "The visibility is bad," says Paumolle. "I don't think it's going to be any better than this all day," says Jaurena. He gives him back the bowl, and Paumolle returns to the galley, tumbling down the steps of the ladder at high speed. During these downward climbs, when he no longer has to worry about keeping his balance to safeguard the coffee, Paumolle lands only on his heels. This is another kind of game, which, on this morning in particular, doesn't involve any risk, since the ship is more motionless than it would be in a harbor.

In the galley, each time the red bowl comes back, it gets refilled. But on this round Paumolle gets started by drinking the whole bowl on his own, because at this point Quéréjéta is usually sitting on a chest facing the table, in front of a big, white bowl, into which he's crumbled three biscuits. It's customary, after Paumolle has drunk all of his big, red bowl, for him to serve himself a third bowl, into which he too crumbles some sea-biscuits. He lets them swell up in the liquid, during the time it takes to go back up on deck to bring a pail full of coffee to the men on watch. When he comes back down from the deck for the second time, Paumolle eats his breakfast.

As this is happening, the rest of the crew is getting up. For the past six days, since they've been becalmed, they haven't been in any hurry; they've had the time to do nothing. It's Gorri the Red who wakes up the whole gang. He shares a separate compartment with Baléchat, next to the mess. As soon as the light of dawn fills his porthole, he drums on the wooden wall and occasionally lets out two or three incomprehensible yells. But the aroma of the fresh coffee is even more persuasive than he is. The men get up and come straight into the mess, in their boots and their oilskin monkey jackets.

Marchais is the only member of the gang who performs one ablution in particular: he rinses his teeth. He fills his mouth with a glassful of water, gargles, with his lips closed, then sprays the water onto the floor. Each of the others, Hervéou, Archigard, and Roland, combs his beard and moustache, rubs his eyes without washing them, blows his nose, and loads his pipe. Bernard and Libois sprinkle water over the floor of the mess and begin to sweep. The master carpenter sleeps in. But he's waiting for the others to leave so he can start whistling love songs to himself in a forlorn whistle that goes off-key even for "Le Temps de cerises."

The sailor on coffee duty goes to the galley with his zinc bucket. To begin with, for the morning coffee, they'd used a huge tureen, which Brodier was especially adept at delivering while running barefoot at high speed through the passageways and up the ladder. But it broke during the heavy weather last December. Now they use a zinc bucket, which, they say, gives the coffee an unpleasant taste. This doesn't stop them from drinking it all down. Right after they've had their coffee and eaten their sea-biscuits, they go up on deck, and then the men of the last night watch come down and settle into their bunks.

There's nothing more to do today than there has been for the past week. The ship is at a dead standstill in the sea, whose surface is extraordinarily metallic, pressed up against the hull like molten lead. The water is steaming on every side in the heavy rain. Baléchat relieves Monsieur Jaurena as commander of the watch, and Archigard takes the wheel, which he holds for a moment with his knee, long enough to tap out his just-extinguished pipe and load a fresh one. Anyway, as it is, the wheel stays perfectly motionless. At most, it creaks occasionally, without moving. At the foot of the mainmast, between two rows of stacked crates, the men have stretched a tarpaulin, where they come right away to shelter and sit down. The rain is drenching the deck, which lies so level at times the water collects in big, deep puddles without running left or right. Then a slight rocking of the ship makes this rainwater flow to one side or the other and it runs, like a stream, the whole length of the deck.

The sails, all of them unfurled in order to catch the least breath of wind, are so heavy with rain, at the slightest movement of the ship, the masts creak from top to bottom. Sometimes, even without any movement, the yards groan in their collars. The rain drums endlessly on the sails.

The shelter the men have made for themselves between the crates is about two meters wide; inside, they've put four or five sea-biscuit boxes, which they use as benches and tables. They sit hunched over in their boots and oilskins and at first, without taking off their sou'westers, they try to play cards. From time to time Archigard steps out to get some air. As soon as he leaves the shelter, the rain starts spattering on his clothes, and he strides in his heavy boots through the puddles as far as the quarterdeck.

The sun is up, but you can't see more than ten meters in any direction. It's still overcast, just as it was at dawn. The rain isn't coming down in squalls, but nonstop, vertically, like a sounding line.

But they can't see a thing. On all sides, the sea is steaming in the rain. Going aft to the quarterdeck also gives them the opportunity to pass beside the wheelhouse and look through the glass panes at the helmsman, who's smoking his pipe next to the motionless wheel. What they'd like to see is that he finally has his hands raised to steer. But, every time, they see him with his arms hanging by his sides, standing next to his wheel. Marchais has already been through weather like this. It was in 1923, he says, more than 3,000 miles west of here, off the island of Tova. They were becalmed for more than two weeks, a few cable lengths from the shore, by weather so dense, they couldn't even see the beacon on the island's summit. Despite the soundings, they went on thinking they were out on the open sea, and didn't suspect the island was so close. But they were puzzled by a muffled sound coming uninterrupted from up ahead, which turned out to be nothing more than the sound of the rain in the bushes. During this whole, calm period, he said, the prow didn't shift any farther than the breadth of a playing card; and they were held fast, more surely than by an anchor, by the weight of the rain.

They keep quiet and listen to the crackling on the tarpaulin stretched overhead, and to the crashing of bucketsful of rainwater, which the slightest rocking of the ship launches against the side walls.

When he returns from one of these walks, Archigard undoes his chin strap and slaps his sou'wester against his boot. He says he, too, once saw a rain nearly the same as this, but on land. He was back home on leave. Shepherds' horns were sounding from the mountains all around, and there wasn't one tree in the forest that wasn't shivering from head to foot, as if someone had told it some dreadful news. Streams had swollen high enough to flood the gardens, and water was starting to overflow the thresholds of houses, even though, in his part of the country, they're always raised three steps above the ground. A nasty business, he says. And with that, he carefully dries his beard and his moustache, rubbing them for a long while from left to right, and from right to left, with the back of his hand. "The funny thing was," he says, "my reason for coming home was to get out and relax in the countryside, and the kind of nature I wanted to see, more than anything else, was ripe grain. Golden grain. That's the kind of nature I'd have been delighted to see. Because, in our sailor's trade, even though there's no lack of nature, you don't find much straw-colored yellow out at sea. As it happens, where I come from, there's no wheat. What there is, is rye. But, rye or wheat, what I wanted to see was ripened grain, dried grain and dust. I had a longing to see dust too. I remembered, back in the day, when I was an apprentice blacksmith with the farrier in my village, I saw lanes full of dust and ripe grain. For more than six months, I'd been longing to see some dust and some ripe grain. And on my first day back, when I arrived at the station and took the bus, it was raining; I got off the bus and walked up to my home through a driving rain. I stayed for ten days. It didn't stop raining for one minute. I went out more than twenty times to go and see the fields of rye. You couldn't say they weren't yellow. They were, but they were knocked down by the rain and so muddied, they no longer had anything in common with the yellow of a field of rye under full sunshine. So I left. It was still raining, I caught the bus, it was raining, and it was only from the train, near Sète, that I saw some sun. But, at that point, the train passed through vineyards sprayed with sulfur, blue enough to make you vomit. Right after, we came into Sète, and then the train crossed over a sort of dike with the sea on both sides. Well, this is how I didn't get to satisfy my longing to see some dust and some ripe rye."

Archigard is twenty-seven years old. His hair and his bushy beard are black and curly. He has very thick eyebrows. Between his eyebrows and his hair, you see only a fingerbreadth of forehead. The skin on his forehead is almost black, too, completely sunburned. It even looks like his eyes are set at the level of his hair. They're lovely, admirable, wide eyes, clear and bright. They make him look like some sort of magical beast. His beard is so thick, and its color so dense, you can see neither his mouth nor his chin. His pug nose barely sticks out past his moustache. This makes it seem like his whole face consists of nothing but eyes. The rest of him is massively powerful. But in contrast to Hervéou, who's equally renowned for his strength and carries a gigantic body with his hefty legs, Archigard has unusually broad shoulders and a flat belly; no doubt, Paumolle, who has the biggest hands of anyone in the crew, can stretch his thumb and index finger halfway around Archigard's waist. Even in rubber boots, Archigard has a flowing stride. He absorbs each step with his knees. When he was hired on board, he didn't have such a thick beard as he does now. Then, you could see, behind his beard, his small mouth: pink, thin-lipped, and sad. This mouth would extinguish all the light of his eyes. As his beard grew and masked the sadness of his lips, his eyes, which remained just the same as they'd been before, grew extremely joyful.

He never takes part directly in a conversation. He shows up. He listens, and he starts talking to himself in a sort of long monologue suggested to him by the conversation he's just heard. The others are used to this and they listen to him. The pleasure they get from listening to him always comes from the contrast between what he's saying and the joyful light in his eyes. When he talks, you don't see his mouth, and the beard that covers it makes all his words whistle slightly. He's extremely brave and calm. His movements are slow but precise. He executes all his orders to completion without any clumsiness. When he's finished with what he's been ordered to do, he will absolutely not undertake anything on his own initiative, but awaits further orders. He's never the first to talk, he never sings, he can stay silent indefinitely. He has a prodigious ability to listen and an infallible memory.

He came on board very badly equipped. At that point he had a denim boilersuit, some espadrilles, and an old pea jacket. Like the other men, he was given some new clothes. But they couldn't find any shirts with shoulders wide enough. Even Hervéou's are too tight. Archigard has enlarged his own shirts with triangles of blue cloth he's cut from his boilersuit.

Gorri the Red shows up. He's a short man, skinny, exuberant, and ever so blond. His blondness is startling. He has the look of a dark-skinned southerner. Nevertheless, he's blond, like linen—almost white—and it's this blondness over this unexpected body that got him the nickname: the Red. He disappears under his huge oilskin. He doesn't wear a sou'wester, but he's made himself a sort of hood out of sailcloth, and tightens it around his face with a braided drawstring that runs through a hem. Out of this his small face emerges, wrinkled like an old apple, and very blond. Most of all, his long, soft moustache, which hangs down on either side of his mouth. He shaves his cheeks and his chin with care. Over his bunk, in the little cubicle he shares with Baléchat, he's hung two family photographs. One of them is very old. It's obvious it shows him, on his marriage day, surrounded by the whole wedding party; he's sitting beside his wife, whose right little finger he has hooked in his left little finger. In this picture he's innocent and rosy-cheeked, with a handsome, chubby face. His moustache, which was barely starting to grow at that time, doesn't yet hide the two dimples at the corners of his mouth. He must be wearing a fine, navy-blue suit, which, in the photograph, looks black, and on his knees he's carefully placed a wide-brimmed boater he doesn't dare touch out of fear he might dirty the straw. His wife is proudly decked out in white from head to toe, and since she's bony and dark-haired, she resembles a fly in a glass of milk. What you notice most about her at first glance are her huge, peasant's hands, one of which is resting idly on her knees, the other hooked by her little finger onto Gorri's. But, sitting to the right of her son, is the most adorable, diminutive old woman, in a white, fluted headdress. She's dressed in black and adorned with jet jewelry. Her embroidery is studded with black pearls, which gleam in the photograph. Even though she's no bigger than a grasshopper, she sits very proudly on her chair. She must have been staring at the photographer, her eyes widened with a sort of fear heightened by the exceptional solemnity of this occasion. At this moment you see nothing of her under her fluted headdress except for a pair of enormous eyes and an anxious little lurch that suddenly shifts her, just now, toward her son. Around these three characters sit their fat, self-satisfied cousins, grocers and butchers from a village in the Morvan.

The second photo tacked above Gorri's bed is another family portrait; but this time, what you see is a first communion. Gorri has been relegated to the second row. His upper body is visible behind his wife and daughter. This time it's his daughter who's decked out in white. She's a fair-haired little mouse, with crafty eyes and a sharp nose, who clenches her lips. She was playing with the strap of her purse when the photographer caught her by surprise. At this moment Madame Gorri must have said to her "Sit up straight," because you can see the mother's lips have moved and her mouth is smudged, while her face is still bony. Even so, around her nose, time has hollowed out two or three creases, which the photographer has clumsily tried to erase. By that day, Gorri was already the man he is today. His long moustache has covered up his childish dimples, and you can tell his skin has been tanned by many suns. The same relations are gathered around him, except for the diminutive old woman with the fluted headdress, who's disappeared from the crowd. But, next to the fat butcher cousin, there's now a young woman with a large bun. An enormous lace collar, reinforced with stays, holds her head upright. She's corseted, squeezed tight, and inflated with huge breasts and buttocks.

Gorri never talks about his family. Gorri never talks about a wife, a daughter, or parents.

When you listen to Gorri, it's an unmarried loner who's talking, a single man possessed by a single passion: a passion for suns! He knows all the suns that can light up the earth, at every point on its surface. From the sun that suffuses the tips of icebergs in the Kara Sea with pink, to the sun that tints the tips of icebergs in the Gerlache Strait with green, to the thousand fiery spheres that warm the continents, the oceans, and the seas, over the entire globe. It's something you have to understand once and for all: Gorri never talks about the sun in the singular. Gorri has formed a family of suns with whom he lives.

Nevertheless, so many suns haven't darkened his skin. He still has his fair complexion, freckled around his nose, and his eyes have remained lashless and lidless, as if he'd always inhabited a cave.

He has an elegant style of command. Although he always makes sure they're effective, his maneuvers are adorned with subtle flourishes. When he's in command, the men carry out maneuvers like dancers performing an imaginary task. The sail drops, the reef is tied up, the wheel changes the ship's heading with precision. But all of this is performed rhythmically, breathlessly.

Baléchat calls out from the forecastle. "Archigard, come here and take a look," he says, "you and the one with you." He's standing there, half-obscured by the rain, like a glistening cask. Gorri the Red also comes and joins the two men Baléchat has summoned. Baléchat leads them to the prow. This is at a moment when the rain is falling harder and heavier. "So, have a look," he says, "it seems like we're turning on the spot." The men lean over. Archigard even hangs out halfway over the rail, having lashed himself to a windlass rope. "It's our bow," Baléchat says, "take a look and see if it isn't turning in this direction."

It's a barely perceptible movement, but maybe Baléchat is right. Whatever the case may be, there's certainly no forward progress: the water, though it's bubbling under the rain, is sealed hermetically around the stem. But on the port side of the prow, there's a tiny ripple, and on the starboard side, an eddy. And in front of these, a ridge of water raised by the stem itself as it shifts.

"Right, go see the helmsman," says Archigard to Brodier, "and get a move on, boy. Ask if he can feel anything through his gauntlets."

Brodier is the youngest member of the crew. He's barely twenty. They'd call him the "cabin boy" if that name could really go along with his gigantic dimensions. He's a sort of pallid giant, who's never been known to eat his fill, and couldn't ever possibly eat his fill, even at the most sumptuous wedding feast. Hence this slackness, this sagging of his legs and arms, and this paleness, which makes him look as though he lives inside too big a skin. Despite his huge bones, which are visible along the whole length of his arms, and his huge knees, each of which is bigger than a man's head (they astonished the other sailors when he undressed on the first night in the forecastle), his bones would have to be twice as big, plus he'd have to grow enormously fat, to completely fill out his skin. His skin doesn't appear to have any connection with his being. It seems too far removed from his blood; a papery grey skin that no amount of scrubbing could whiten. And besides, his features show the signs of premature aging and weakness typical of giants.

He goes off toward the quarterdeck, slapping his big feet down in all the puddles. "What do you expect me to be able to feel through a device like this?" says the helmsman, striking the wheel with the flat of his hand. The wheel seems absolutely disengaged and it turns effortlessly. "It's been a long while since it stopped steering, my friend. What does Baléchat think we're up to? Does he think I'm adjusting the clocks? Is there any way I can know if his boat is slipping through the water at all? Look, I can't feel a thing with this helm, it's spinning like a top. What's he going on about, your Baléchat? It looks to me like we're moving sideways, sideways to port. We're completely planted adrift. Tell him that for me, and tell him to stop spinning us yarns."

Brodier finds them leaning over the port rail, almost at the foot of the mainmast. They've come this far aft, following the same, folded ripple in the water below. It's not a severe drift, but it is one.

"Has anyone seen the officers?" says Archigard. "What the hell do you expect the officers to do in weather like this?" asks Gorri. "I'm going to the lab. Anyway, if I were in their place, I know just what I'd do." "And what is it you'd do?" asks Baléchat. "I'd stay nice and dry with my pipe.

Baléchat is uneasy. By nature. He doesn't need anything external to happen; he can stir up his anxiety on his own. He's rotund, like a ball, with short legs and arms. Often he stays completely still, like he's lying in wait. And, as a matter of fact, he is lying in wait. After a minute he rubs his nose with his index finger. As far as he's concerned, nothing is natural. Nature itself isn't natural. It can only be understood as a threat, which can reside just as well in silence and shadows as it can in light, by day or by night.

Baléchat reformulates his problem all the time. Ever since he was born, up until today, he hasn't even begun to work out the solution. Until now he's been content to go on endlessly varying the terms of the proposition. He's forced, constantly, to vary the terms of the problem. There are constantly new things that alter and exacerbate the meaning of the test that's been set for him.

If it's quiet, why is it quiet? If it's daytime, why is it daytime? Furthermore, why night? And why noise? And why all of it?

Motionless, he listens, then rubs his nose with his index finger.

But if a real event happens to transpire, then Baléchat, no longer asking himself any questions, acts with astounding swiftness. There's never been a case where this roly-poly body with the limbs of an insect hasn't hurled himself straight into the heart of the matter, with more speed and agility than any athlete. His orders are clear and concise, and he expects them to be carried out with such promptness, even as he's issuing them, he leaps forward with vehemence to perform what he's ordered the others to do. At such times, while he's commanding and taking action, he seems to be giving a synthesis of the situation and its solutions. In that moment, he's endowed with an acute sense of precision. Even if he were blind (and there are situations where the darkness in which he struggles is equivalent to total sightlessness), his foot would always be the first to land on the required spot, and his hand the first to grasp, right away, with machine-like precision, the thing that needs to be done without delay. Once the deed is done, he never harks back on what has happened, either to draw conclusions, or to rejoice, or to regret. He goes on, motionless and mute, viewing nature with grave suspicion.

Gorri heads toward the oceanography and zoology labs. They're both in a deckhouse that's installed forward of the main hatch and extends as far as the mizzen mast. Monsieur Hour and Monsieur Trocelier settle in there first thing in the morning. Trocelier comes up, wrapped in a worn mackintosh, the legacy of some old uncle; it's extremely useful, because it's warm and roomy at once. Hour has remained faithful to his wool sweater and pea coat. When he comes into the lab, he hangs his coat on the stand, and keeps his sweater on while he prepares all his samples. Trocelier, by contrast, tightens his mackintosh around his waist with a strap and, rolling his sleeves up past his wrists, handles his test tubes with the air of an old monk in a distillery.

Usually, Gorri comes to spend the first hours of the morning with them. Gorri is interested in all the natural flotsam Hour dissects, classifies, and catalogues. There are different sizes and colors of feathers, which bring to mind the birds of all the world's oceans and bays. These feathers are classified and inserted upright into slots in the pages of cardboard registers. When Gorri slowly turns them in the morning, each of these pages is like a congregation of birds from the shores of every ocean. Hour has also classified hair from the coats and furs of aquatic and terrestrial mammals. You can imagine them coming out of their lairs, diving from reefs, sinking their teeth into prey, nursing their young, or perishing, bloodied, in extraordinary struggles over food. So far Gorri has only glanced at the albums containing tufts of fur, which are glued on, or the patches of skin, which are laid in to the paper. But he's delighted to know that, once he's finished going through the feathers, when he no longer enjoys sending the phantom flock of catalogued birds soaring over the seas every morning, he'll be able to move on to evoking, through their coats, all the shore-dwelling mammals. Hour also has collections of scales, ranging from the minuscule, tinier than the head of a pin, to the huge, as wide as the palm of your hand. Finally, he has a thick album he calls a seaweed herbarium, where he's assembled a phantasmagoria of colors and shapes, which enchant Gorri's eye and frighten him: every sort of seaweed he's encountered in his intertwining voyages around the globe. In the zoology lab, there's always a big tub where some transparent grasses are being treated. In a little while, glued to a sheet of paper, they'll become new crystals in the phantasmagoria that enchants the boatswain.

But Monsieur Hour has barely just arrived. Before he gets down to work this morning, like every morning, two ceremonies take place in the zoology lab. Hour is a young man, dark-haired, tanned, lean, and dreamy. Long voyages have left their mark in his eyes and on his forehead and have darkened his skin. He has long, busy hands, tawny like a Creole's. As he does every morning, he takes from his drawer an album with locking metal clasps, which he opens with a tiny key that hangs like a charm from his watch chain. It's a photo album. Hour is an only son. Like some very rare men, he has only a mother. The album contains photos of her starting from when she was a boarder at the lycée for girls in Amiens, up until now, when she's living in a small, suburban house in Arcueil. Every morning Hour begins his mother's life again and reviews it in its entirety, from the days of her glazed cotton schoolgirl's smock, till those of her white hair and jet-black kerchief. Meanwhile, Gorri is looking through the third volume, devoted to the white feathers of Atlantic seabirds.

The oceanography lab is separated from the zoology lab by a plain, wooden partition. You can hear Monsieur Trocelier in there, tapping his pipe on the palm of his hand. Then he takes a series of long, heavy breaths, since he makes a habit of beginning each day with deep, controlled breathing exercises. He's a full-bodied, clean-shaven man with a flushed complexion, who has great confidence in routine. He's an expert on the Bay of Bengal and the China Sea. Next, you can hear him uncork a flask, into which he pours, every week, his seven days' ration of whisky. After that, silence falls on the side of the oceanography lab.

"It seems," says Gorri, "we're completely planted adrift." Monsieur Hour is looking at his mother's wedding photograph. Even though the windows of the lab are closed, you can hear the captain whistling below-decks—as he does every morning—a tune from Mozart's *Flute Concerto*.

It was an actual drift. Aside from the material facts that bore it out, there was the feeling they were no longer in control and were being swept sideways. The days dragged on, in this rain that shrouded the view in all directions. Most of the time the men stayed in the shelter they'd made under the tarpaulin between two rows of crates. Up above on the poop, behind the glass panes of his little enclosure, they could see the face of the helmsman. He was daydreaming, with nothing to do. But, every once in a while, he'd turn his glance to the port side, where they felt they were being swept away. In the shelter, the crew were also looking in that direction.

They felt this drift most distinctly the moment they stretched out in their bunks. If it was daytime, you felt right away you were being pushed gently toward the partition wall, or that you were slipping out of your berth on the sly. The rain had been drumming relentlessly for days and days, endlessly heavy and impenetrable. Occasionally a heavy bootstep would sound on the deck, making its way slowly, like the tread of a lone man wandering through the corridors of a deserted castle. Or else, amid the hammer blows of the rain, you'd hear a low groan coming from the heel of the mainmast. Then, if you were in bed belowdecks, despite the gloom that prevailed there at all times, you'd notice a subtle shift in the outlines of the bulkheads and storage compartments. The floor itself, though hidden in shadows, would be slowly lifting and falling. These were clear manifestations of the force that was sweeping the ship away in an irresistible drift. As soon as you went back up on deck, the rainfall was so dense and regular, it seemed like you were underneath the overflow of a more elevated sea draining into the one below. If, by chance, a little, distant daylight—which you'd forgotten about, but which must be illuminating the earth—succeeded in slipping under the raging curtains of rain, then you saw that the masts were completely black with dampness, and that the sails themselves were completely black, as if each of them had been carved out of ebony.

At night the silence would awaken the men with a start. For days and days the rain had been roaring so regularly without letup, their ears, grown accustomed to uninterrupted rumblings, took them for silence. Each man, as he awoke, tried to listen to see if he could hear, at long last, the tramping of feet engaged in maneuvers. But each time it was still only this roaring silence; once in a while there was the creaking of the heel of the mast, or the squeaking of a lantern overhead swinging from its hook.

At dawn Archigard tumbled barefoot from the galley and came to shout in the forecastle: "We can see, boys, we can see, come quick!" Then he ran to the officers' wardroom. The men came up on deck. The whole watch was leaning over the starboard rail, looking at something abeam. The helmsman had his face glued to the glass pane of his enclosure.

It was there, in the murky light of dawn, abeam, but ahead, because they were being pushed toward it: a sort of dark mass, at the surface of the water, in the smoking rain. It must have been barely two cable lengths away. As they were listening, they suddenly heard a dull, plunging sound, as though a wave had just broken onto a reef. Baléchat, on watch, raced up to the helm, but they could see him up there trying to steer in vain. The captain and the two officers had no sooner emerged from the companionway than Baléchat cried out to them: "A reef, messieurs!" while pointing his finger toward the object, "We're being driven on to it!" The captain hadn't taken the time to put on his oilcloth; he was in his dressing gown and slippers, bareheaded under the rain shower. He wiped the rain off his face, shaded his eyes with the flat of his hand, and came forward to the rail. The men made way for him.

"There's no reef in that vicinity," he said coolly to Monsieur Larreguy. "No, monsieur," said Larreguy. "Where are we, approximately?" "About two thousand miles southeast of Cape Virgines, monsieur, as best I could plot."

The drift was imperceptible, and contrary to logic, the reef against which they'd been gradually driven seemed to be receding and fading from sight. But this could have been a trick of the mist.

"No steerage way?" cried the captain to the helm. "Not even a gram," answered Balèchat. "Launch a dinghy to port, we'll try to warp ourselves with a mooring line. Stay here," he said to Messieurs Larreguy and Jaurena, "I'm going down to get my oilskin." In fact, his woolen dressing gown was already soaking wet.

Monsieur Larreguy left three men on the lookout on the starboard side, to report if the possible reef, which had melted into the rain, were to come into view. The small rowboat was immediately launched to port, and the crew made up of Archigard, Paumolle, Bernard, Brodier, and Libois, with Gorri in command, began pulling hard to make as much headway as possible to the west.

All at once the rowboat itself disappeared in the rain. Finally, it must have reached the end of the mooring line. The men on the ship began to haul on the cable, which became taut. Slowly, the prow began to swing to the west, and soon, with the efforts of the rowers, it moved forward slowly in that direction. It was the first time in more than twenty days they'd started to make headway again.

Abruptly, the cable slackened, and on board they could hear somebody hailing from the dinghy. It was impossible to make out what they were trying to say. All you could hear was Gorri's voice. After crying out, he'd started talking to the men on the ship, trying to explain something that had just happened. At the same time, you could hear the oars of the dinghy, on its way back, getting louder. It broke through the mist of the rain. Gorri was standing up in the stern. He let the dinghy draw in until he placed his hand on the ship's hull. Monsieur Larreguy leaned over to him. "The reef is out in this direction," Gorri said. "If I keep rowing ahead, instead of towing you away, I'll pull you right on to it. We can hear the waves crashing, loud and clear." Baléchat came out of the wheelhouse. "Then there must be two of them," he said, "because from where I am, up here, I can see one to starboard as well." "At a hundred meters," said Gorri, "at a hundred meters to port, I reached the end of the cable, and then I pulled another twenty strokes, and we saw it as plain as the nose on your face. We could even make out the breakers all around. At the north tip, there's one jagged rock in particular that juts far out from the backwash." "There is no backwash," said Larreguy. Indeed, the sea was still so calm, so flat, Gorri didn't hesitate to lean against the side of the ship, as though it were lying in harbour. "And besides," said Larreguy, "we're not in the vicinity of any atoll. No, we're at 50° latitude in the open Atlantic Ocean. Reefs don't just turn up by the grace of God."

At this very moment, Archigard cried out that a reef was coming into view, a cable length ahead.

This one, all the men could see. In a stupor, they didn't realize right away it was coming closer to the ship on its own, fairly quickly, swaying from side to side, dark, gleaming, rain-spattered, edged with cresting waves, and revolving like a top, which was extraordinary for a reef. Finally, under their very eyes, it slid away off their beam and submerged completely, with a sombre gurgle, into a whirlpool, out of which emerged the streaming tail of a whale. Gorri had figured out what it was right away. He and his crew climbed back on deck and hauled up the dinghy.

All day long, from one moment to the next, they spotted a large number of whales in every direction. Despite the pounding of the rain, they could hear them slapping the water with their tails, spouting, and sloshing seawater in their throats. Sometimes they would break through the grey haze of the rain and appear, sailing peacefully through the quiet water, as if they intended to ram the side of the ship with their foreheads. But every time, as lively as carp, each one sheered away with a flick of the tail and slid almost noiselessly alongside the ship, so close to the rail, you could have jumped onto its back.

This idea had occurred immediately to Paumolle. Paumolle was a man who thrived on taking dizzying risks. Each time he climbed into the rigging, once he was above the mainsail yard and the deck below looked no bigger than a little olive, he yearned to be in the grip of danger. He'd cling one way or another to the mainstay, or else he'd sit right down astride the slippery yard, and even during the most violent swaying of the rigging, especially during the most violent swaying, he yearned to suddenly release his hands in order to experience that electrifying sensation of the onset of death.

On certain evenings, smoking his pipe, he would explain this impulse to Libois. Libois would sit, calmly chewing his wad, not saying a word. Now and then he'd squirt some golden saliva into his hands. Paumolle would talk about that onset of death.

"Neither of us" he said, "is at any risk whatsoever in the rigging. I must have climbed at least a thousand kilometers of masts and ropes and cables. It's a boulevard. But when I let go of my hands—and you know, you can hardly hang on to a spar with just your thighs—the yard swings around, and what's more, on the port side it hangs out over the mizzenmast boom. You feel like you aren't holding on to anything." "You'll break your neck," said Libois. "Maybe I'll break my neck, but I can't stop myself from starting the plunge. Of course, I stop myself, but just in time. Have you ever been up in high storeys?" "What storeys?" asked Libois. "Of a building." "What building?" "Tall ones." "Where?" asked Libois. "In cities." "Yes, I have," said Libois. "As high as the sixth storey?" "Yes," said Libois. "So, where?" "In Villeurbanne." "When I'm up that high, I have the urge to climb on top of the balcony railing. And one time I did. We were celebrating my sister's marriage. They made me get down, but I came back that night. "What do you want?" my mother asked. I said, "I'm going to get my jacket." I went into the bedroom, I opened the window, and I swung my leg up over the railing. I jammed my toes into an opening in the ironwork. That night, down below, the boulevard was full of cars and headlights gliding along, and up above the street, the lights of the stars looked almost the same. I let my hands go ten times. I was only holding on with the tips of my toes. It was amazing. My mother called out. "What are you up to in there?" "Nothing." I climbed back down from the railing, put on my jacket, gave my mother a kiss, and I left. I walked around all night and never went to bed. I said to myself: "Paumolle, you have to sign on to a ship, on the double."

Jumping onto a whale's back should be simple. But it's not something you should try it in rubber boots that slip and slide. Maybe he'll put on some shore shoes with cleats, maybe some espadrilles, or maybe he'll just go barefoot. The whales are passing within two meters of the ship. One of them has come close to scraping against the hull. You jump, you stay upright, and the fish takes you away. The ship isn't moving, so you can always swim back. You should be able to go at least a hundred meters standing on top of the creature. It would hardly know you were there. Once it veers away from the ship, it speeds off on the surface in the rain. Perhaps, out there, it dives, or perhaps it keeps on circling slowly and wouldn't be worrying about what's on its back. It's a simple matter of balance. You have to keep yourself standing on the slippery skin. It shouldn't be any more difficult than keeping upright on the deck in foul weather. You must have to face forward, shifting your weight back and forth from left to right.

If the whale dives, you have to go down with the whirlpool, without struggling, as though you're lifeless, holding your breath until the eddies settle and spread. Then all you have do is swim back to the ship. If you slip off while you're riding, you just end up in the water. It's easy, and Paumolle really wants to do it.

"What the hell do you want us to be doing here? It's raining. Do you have any idea where the sea is dragging us? We can't see a thing up ahead, behind, on the right, or on the left. The rain is hanging like a curtain all around. It's a kind of blurry, moving wall, and the most unexpected things can appear through it at any time. But it often hangs around us for ages without moving, not letting anything through, other than a hazy light in which nothing ever happens.

"It's impossible to know where we'll be tomorrow. The spot where we were planted in the sea yesterday is exactly like the one we're planted in today, and the spot where we'll be planted in the sea tomorrow will be exactly like the one we're planted in now. The little ripple that's swelling up on our port side will be exactly the same. The pitter-patter of the rain will roll on just the same, and the curtains of rain that are closing us in on all sides will be exactly the same as they are now, dark and blue, throbbing and heavy, closed in every direction.

"What we want is a breath of wind. We want to see this black sail start to swell and shake off all the rain it's soaked with, we want the mast to stop creaking in its step and we want it to start squealing from its spars and its trucks, the way it does when the wind catches it head-on. We want to hear the mainsail flap and watch it unfurl like a snake, while it swells on one side and flutters on the other like a flag in the wind, and then billows out. We want the sails to be full at last, from the heads of the masts to their feet. We want the wind to press straight down on the whole spread of our canvas on all three masts, from top to bottom, and for us to be racing ahead at last, bow forward. It's not that we want the rain to stop falling. And it's not that we no longer want to be wrapped in dark veils, where anything can loom up at any time but nothing ever happens in the end, except in tiny drips, far apart from each other. We can put up with the rain and with being shut up inside the dark walls of mist, but we want to be able to steer.

"We wouldn't mind if we were lost in these barren stretches of three thousand, four thousand, or thousands of thousands of miles, but we want to be able to steer.

"We couldn't care less if the sea went on forever covered in rain, yesterday, today, and tomorrow; we could put up with all that; we could even put up with never seeing anything other than the tip of our prow pushing back a lip of water on either side; what we want, more than anything, is to be able to steer, because to steer gives us the certainty that we're just as alive as the rain and the sea; and in that case, it wouldn't matter that the endless reaches of the sea lie under the endless hissing of the rain; if, precisely, we ourselves, in the midst of all of it, were able to steer. Because this little world we dwell in is ruled by the wheel. If we say: 15 degrees right, we point the bow 15 degrees to the right, and we don't care if it's so dense and overcast that we can't tell right from left, or one degree from the length of a boot. What we need is to steer; not toward anything; and even if there's no longer a right or a left, or a zero, or a degree, or a 'like this,' there's the ability to steer, and that fact is as important as the great, endless ocean reaches and the endless downpouring of the rain, so that you might act, get to the heart of things, and hold on to the feeling of liberty.

Even if there were no shore beyond the rain, even if you weren't steering toward any destination, there is the action of steering and there are all the places to which you point the prow when you give the order: right, left, let out sail, turn downwind, run free, put down the helm; all the places the prow points to are immediately, in that very moment, shores you reach and ports you enter through instantaneous flashes that last for eternities.

"Simply because you're steering, you reach them in that very moment; you possess, you travel, you move; movement immediately fulfils our high hopes.

"Even when the sky is empty and the sea is empty. When you're moving through a hollow opening in the sky, so vast, only one perceptible movement remains, that of the sun going from west to east; when, despite the active wheel and the view that can encompass all the points of the circle of the horizon at all times, you still find yourself fixed in the same place, in a wake that begins and never ends; at the very least, you do have the sensation of heading toward something. Even if the nakedness of the sea succeeds the nakedness of the sea day after day, you're making headway toward something, and you're doing the most important thing a man can do: even without purpose or reason, you're making headway.

"Nothing can make your courage falter when you're making headway.

"Everything opens up, and you get to the heart of everything; you do the thing for which we were brought to life: you steer toward something, and even if you're steering toward nothing, you're steering! The journey takes place, whatever it may be, and that's the only thing that counts.

"So you'd put up with the gloomy banners of rain, and even the lid of water that fits tightly over the great plate of the water of the sea. You'd put up with being pressed between the two watery millstones, as long as, in spite of it all, you could make headway and steer, and hear them saying: right, left, zero, or 'like this,' indicating in this way that there is a right, a left, a clear direction that defines us and makes us exist.

"The rain is nothing, and the immense reaches of the sea are nothing. The whole sky could become a waterfall, from top to bottom, and bring the sea to a boil. The sky could become a cascade of fire, or collapse like granite and hollow out the whirlpool of the black abyss around us. The sea itself could leap into the sky, like thousands of whales; from the moment you steer, in the midst of the most dreadful cataclysm, there's a right, a left, a good and a bad road; you're making headway; you continue to perform, imperturbably—on the good road or the bad road—the most important action that man can perform, since it's essentially the one for which he was put on earth.

"But we aren't steering. The wheel of the helm is wild, free, it doesn't weigh an ounce, it can't act, either to the right or to the left, it's spinning. What we're making isn't headway, it's an immobility that's carrying us away without moving ; we can't act. To do what we're doing, it isn't necessary to have been born; a shipwreck would follow the same route. It's not a question here of life or death, it's a question of the most terrifying thing a man can imagine: to be inanimate."

This is why all the men on the ship are hastening to find a soul within themselves.

Translator's Acknowledgments

Jill Schoolman embraced this project with insight and enthusiasm. The staff at Archipelago Books have been a pleasure to work with. *Mille mercis à vous tous!*

The gratitude I owe to Jacques Le Gall is inexpressible. Isabelle Génin has been unfailingly generous with her commentary and astute advice. Agnès Castiglione gave me wise and timely encouragement.

Edmund White's appreciation continues to propel me forward.

Among my readers, I want particularly to thank Roo Borson, Wendell Block, Peter Sakuls, Mark Silverman, Paul Clifford, Tim Brook, David Boote, Roy Pelletier, and Deirdre Newman. With her sensitive feedback, Debbie Honickman has helped to improve the translation at every stage.

Sylvie Durbet-Giono, to whom her father had promised to dedicate *Fragments d'un Paradis* (but, as she likes to say with a note of playful regret, "*il a oublié!*"), has imbued me with a profound sense of connection. While I'd like to remedy, in part, her father's lapse, I also want to honour the memory of Jacques Mény, tireless champion of *Les Amis de Jean Giono*, without whose support I wouldn't have embarked, in the first place, on this enthralling voyage into the unknown.

Paul Eprile